BLAYZE

A HOPE CITY NOVEL

KRIS MICHAELS

WWW.KRISMICHAELSAUTHOR.COM

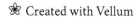 Created with Vellum

CHAPTER 1

Billowing smoke rolled from the front door of the three-story apartment building. Blay King did a final check on his safety equipment and clasped Royal, his partner, on the shoulder. They'd been directed into the building to clear the third floor. Based on a Port Authority cop's report, the first two floors had been cleared and the people who lived in them were accounted for. Approaching the building, he couldn't see flames, but the fire was there, consuming the structure and sending clouds of toxic chemicals into the air.

The exterior team extended the lead attack line from the engine. He and Royal entered the wall of smoke escaping the building and then headed for the stairwell. Bounding up the stairs in full turnout gear wasn't a cakewalk, but he and Royal had trained for this for years, and they knew the risks to the people who might still be up on the third floor. Most people who died in fires died from smoke inhalation. The toxic mix of chemicals in the rolling smoke was deadly, and by the amount of brownish-yellow smoke that billowed down the stairwell... Well, if there were people on the third floor, they didn't have much time.

The heat hit them as they turned on the second-floor landing. By the time they made their way to the third floor, the heat was oppressive but not over-whelming.

Blay spoke for the first time since entering the building. "BC, Team One. We are in the stairwell between the second and third floors. Zero visibility, turning on thermal imaging camera. We need vents ASAP." The BC was the responding Battalion Commander, the man directing on-scene actions.

Blay felt Royal grab his shoulder, and they moved forward. The man pointed up at the blistering paint on the ceiling and shouted, "Heat from above."

He nodded. That's why Royal was such a kick-ass partner. They worked in unison, almost as one person, because they'd trained and worked together for years. Blay reached to the side of his mask, flicking on the small camera that fed thermal images to his in-mask display. "BC, we are on the third floor. Sustained heat from overhead location. Attic or roof." He felt alongside the wall, moving in shuffle steps with Royal at his side. The imaging device was good but it wasn't perfect and wouldn't show him a hole in the floor if he wasn't looking down. Safety was always the first consideration.

"10-4." The BC acknowledged his input and gave orders to the ladder truck to cut vents in the roof. It would give the smoke an escape route and hopefully give them better vision, but if there were people up here, they couldn't wait for the smoke to clear.

His radio crackled, "Team One, Engine 37 Team Two is en route to your location."

"Team One, copy." Blay acknowledged the input. He tried the first door they came to; it was locked. He moved out of the way, and Royal used the W-tool he carried as a twenty-five-pound battering ram and broke in the door. Sweat ran into Blay's eyes and down his back. The inferno above was roasting them like a broiler turned on high sizzled steaks. With the intensity of the heat from the ceiling growing, they wouldn't have much time to clear this floor before they'd have to stop. They cleared the apartment and moved back into the hall just in time to meet up with Team Two from Engine 37.

"This one's clear." Royal yelled the words, and the other team acknowledged him. They cleared two more apartments before Blay's alarm sounded on his oxygen tank. It was set to sound off at forty percent, so they had plenty of oxygen left. Royal's went off a few minutes later. The alarms would let the BC know to call up more inside search personnel.

"Team One, you have ten minutes. Engine 12, send up a replacement search team." The BC's command left little room for argument. They'd clear as much as they could in the time they had left. The team from Engine 37 took the last door on the left, and Blay and Royal took the door on the right. The layout was different than the previous apartment, and there were toys scattered on the floor.

Blay blinked his eyes to clear the sting of sweat. He and Royal scanned and searched the front room, then the kitchen, checking all the cupboards and the pantry. Kids would hide in the darndest places when they were afraid. The bathroom was clear, but the door to the bedroom was swollen shut. Blay was exhausted from being broiled. He leaned back and kicked the door, stumbling inward as the door gave.

Shit!

He nearly fell on his hands and knees. In an attempt to catch himself on the foot of the bed, he saw a body through his thermal imaging camera. "There!" He grabbed Royal's arm and directed him to the corner of the room. On all fours, they found what they were looking for. The smoke made it impossible to assess if the woman was unconscious or dead. Blay crawled past her and cussed: a small child with a wet cloth over their mouth and nose. He took the necessary seconds to pick up the bedspread and scan under the bed and in the closet before he spoke to command.

"BC, Team One."

"Team One, go ahead."

"10-45, one female, one child. Unknown code one or two. Coming down." He gave the information to let the rest of his people know he didn't know if the woman and child were alive or not. He straightened with his small load as Royal strapped the woman to drag her out. In the thick smoke, carrying her was out of the question, but applying the strap around her upper body, he could get her to safety. Blay adjusted the weight of the kid and moved with his partner. He heard Team Two call in another 10-45. *Damn it.*

They worked down the stairwell, Royal going

first, then Blay following in a crouch, keeping the child as low to the ground as possible. He could hear the exterior crews before he could see them. As soon as he appeared through the smoke, the child was whisked out of his arms. He moved to where Royal was bending over, catching his breath. "You good?"

Royal nodded. "Good."

They both stood up and heard the BC's voice over their comms, "Team One, stand down. Team Three is on scene." They both stopped in their tracks. "Engine 58, we have Engine 12 in place. Engine 58, all personnel, fall back behind my vehicle and give me a PAR."

Blay moved toward the rally point, carefully removing his mask and helmet only after clearing the incident site. He and Royal plopped their asses onto the ground and accepted water bottles. Half of his went over his head, and he'd bet good money steam came off him. "Brain fried has a new meaning."

Royal snorted. "It was nuclear. What the fuck was burning up there?"

"Dude, I have no idea." Blay downed the second half of his water. Rocker, their Lieutenant, walked up a couple of minutes later with two more bottles of water. "Good work in there."

"Are they alive?"

"Did they make it?" both Royal and he asked at the same time as they reached for the water.

"The woman, no. Medics are working on the kid."

Blay's stomach lurched. Royal shook his head and muttered, "Fuck."

"We got there as quickly as we could." Blay's words were quiet, for Royal's ears only.

"Doesn't make her any less dead." Royal sighed.

Rocker knelt. "She was probably dead before we pulled up."

Royal nodded. Rocker's words didn't help. The boss man meant well, but two fears were constant when you were on a search team. First, you couldn't get to someone who needed you because sometimes, even with the heat-resistant safety equipment, the temperatures were too high. Second, that somehow it was your fault you didn't get there fast enough. Training reduced the possibility of the first, and nothing mitigated the second. Each firefighter had to deal with the things they saw in their own way. Royal beat himself up mentally and withdrew until he got it straight in his head. He always had. On the other hand, Blay processed everything in the weight room or running. Working out focused him so he could deal with the events of the call.

He glanced up at Rocker. "What about the 10-45 from Team Two?"

The Lieutenant shook his head and stood up. "Haven't heard." Rocker lifted his radio. "BC, this is engine 58. PAR complete. All personnel accounted for."

The Battalion Commander acknowledged the Lieutenant, and the crew mingled around the same area, watching as new replacement teams came in and took over from the crews that had relieved them. Two and a half hours later, the fire was extinguished and the BC terminated the response.

Hokinson, their engineer, oversaw the recovery of their attack hoses. Blay and Royal had used the mobile Cascade system on one of the trucks on the scene to refill their air tanks in case they were needed again. While others worked on emptying the lines, he and Royal also made the rounds to their crew and refilled their air tanks, too. Together, they'd restowed the equipment they'd deployed. The trucks loaded up and left the area one by one, and since they were first on scene, they had to wait until a path was cleared to move the engine. Hokinson was good, but he wasn't a magician.

"We have to stop meeting like this, my man." Sean McBride's voice behind him spun him on his heel.

"Hey. How are you doing?" He extended his hand and smiled at Sean's partner, Jonas.

Sean pulled him in for a hug, slapping his back a couple of times. "I'd be better if I were in bed asleep. Where is the Battalion Commander?"

Blay turned and pointed in the general location. "Behind the ladder truck that's trying to move through."

"Thanks, man. You're going to be at the house on Sunday, right?"

"Yeah, I've been threatened. Hover Mother is adamant we are doing everything in one day."

Sean chuckled. "Between our mothers, if there is a way to finish everything, it will be done."

He snorted. "Ryker and Brie's wedding isn't for a month."

"You'll learn one day. Women take this stuff seriously. We better get over there and get our briefing. Take it easy, kiddo." Sean winked, and he and Jonas headed off to do their job. He and Rory, Sean's brother, were the youngest of the Kings and McBrides and best friends. They'd grown up sharing a massive backyard and practically lived in each other's houses. Their parents were best friends, and sometimes he swore he had ten brothers and sisters instead of four. Rocker whistled, rallying the crew. They clambered back up into the engine for the short ride back to the station.

As Hokinson backed the truck into the station, Blay attached the hose to vent the engine's exhaust. The relief crew would be in at eight, and it was almost six by the time they pulled in. The response was over, but their work wasn't. The turnout gear needed to be cleaned. Theirs wasn't a safe profession for a multitude of reasons. The chemicals in the smoke settled on their gear so making sure the gear was clean was self-preservation. The carcinogens in the smoke and burned, melted building materials could cause cancer.

When the relief crew arrived, Blay hit the showers. He stood under the cool water and let it pour over him. The call-out was the third of the night, and he was dead tired. Twenty-four on, forty-eight off, and he'd end up sleeping like the dead tonight. It was a rare occurrence to get a no-hitter during a shift.

With the other shift on duty, he and the rest of the crew would get dressed in the locker room. It was unwritten code. You cleaned your shit up and got out of the bunk room, even if you had to stick around. He soaped up, rinsed, and dried off. At his locker, he dropped his towel and pulled on his boxer briefs.

"King, are you heading over to the Celtic Cock tonight?" Hokinson asked as he walked past on the way to his locker.

"Man, depends on if I catch some shut-eye." He had a million things to do today, some he dreaded.

"Yeah, I feel yah." Royal yawned as he shuffled out of the showers. "When did we get old?"

"We aren't old. Just well used." Hokinson yawned, too.

Rocker snorted. "Hope City's best-used asset."

Miller and Dorsey exited the showers at the same time. "L.T., did you just call us whores?" Miller held out his fist, and Dorsey bumped it.

The Lieutenant laughed and shook his head. "If the shoe fits, Miller."

The locker room became a back and forth of one-liners at that point. Finally, Blay reached into his locker and turned his phone on. He placed it on the metal bench while he grabbed his street shoes. It damn near exploded as notification after notification pinged and pinged and pinged.

He turned around and looked at the face of the phone, seeing Ellen's name pop up over and over. *Fuck my life.* He dropped his tennis shoes on the floor and sat down as the notifications continued to ping through.

"What the hell, King?" Hokinson's question made him aware everyone in the locker room was looking at him.

He smiled and lifted an eyebrow. "What? Hoke, are you telling me you don't have girls tapping you out when you're on shift?"

"Girls, yes, not an entire nation." The man pointed at the phone, which had finally silenced. "You got a stalker?"

He grunted and bent to put on his shoes. "Something like that." What he had was a *possible* baby momma who was quite possibly insane in the literal sense. He'd spent two nights with her. Two. The last time he made the mistake of taking her to his apartment, and getting her to leave the following day was anything but easy.

"You going to check those messages?" Rocker looked at him from across the way.

Another ding sounded, and he shook his head. "Not now. I'll listen to them on the way home." He wasn't going to spill his dirty laundry at work. He was studying to test for engineer-driver, which came with a hell of a pay raise. He loved what he was doing now, but he had plans—engineer, lieutenant, captain, and battalion chief. Firefighting didn't just run in his veins; it was who he was, down to a cellular level. He'd seen what happened to men and women who brought family problems to work. It distracted the crew, and distractions were something that no one needed in their line of work. Plus, his goal was a promotion, not being pulled into the Captain's office for having a crazy stalker who may be carrying his child.

He tied his shoe and stood up, grabbing his gym bag that held his dirty clothes from the shift. "See you in forty-eight."

"See you tonight at the Cock! Bring your money. My dart-throwing arm needs practice," Hokinson yelled after him.

Dorsey caught up with him and laughed when Blay held up a finger. It would be visible as they walked down the stairs. "See you tonight?"

Blay shrugged and blinked as they walked outside. The May sun was bright and warm. The dogs would love a run. "I'll try, going to see what's up, but probably."

A goofy grin slid across Dorsey's face. "It's been forever since the crew has been trolling together."

Blay snorted out a surprised laugh. "I'm not trolling tonight."

Dorsey smacked him on the arm. "Are you serious? Does the stalker chick have you wrapped around her finger?" Dorsey pointed at the phone in Blay's hand.

"Nah, dude, she's got issues, but I'm seeing someone." Dawn and he had just started dating a month or so ago, right before Ellen dropped the baby bomb. She was his sister-in-law Amber's half-sister and was used to being around cops. Still, there was no way after asking her out fifty times before she finally caved and agreed to go out with him that he would bring her around his crew. Not just yet. He needed to tell her about Ellen, but he was pretty sure that would end in a disaster. Dawn had been damn skittish about dating him because of his reputation as a womanizer. Ellen and her claim that he was the child's father would be a nail in his coffin, but Dawn still needed to know sooner or later, and the way Ellen was ramping up the crazy, it had better be sooner. He wanted to show Dawn he'd changed his partying ways, but Ellen's claims were sidetracking that.

His phone vibrated in his hand. God, had he changed.

"Bring her!" Dorsey started walking backward. "You embarrassed of her?"

"More like I don't want her to meet you guys. You're animals." Blay hit his key fob and unlocked his truck.

Dorsey grabbed his chest. "Oh, damn, that hurt."

"No, it didn't, moron." Blay laughed as Dorsey exaggerated a limp and moaned across the parking lot to his muscle car. He really liked his crew, and yeah, he wanted Dawn to meet them someday.

He got in his truck and rolled down the window before he went to his voice messages.

"Blay, why don't you call me back? You have my number. This is Ellen."

He scrolled to the following message. *"You son of a bitch! You can't ignore me. I'll show you, you bastard."* Her voice snarled with a string of acid-laced curse words.

He scrolled to the next. Ellen sobbed, *"Why don't you love me? You said you love me."*

He listened to the rest of the thirty-two calls. Ellen's mood bounced from happy to furious to weepy to business-like. He dropped his head back on his headrest and stared ahead. The private investigator he'd hired had followed her to an OB appointments and had sweet-talked the receptionist into confirming Ellen was pregnant.

Blay swore under his breath and shook his head slowly. He'd suited up. He always did. There was no way that he'd gotten her pregnant, but he'd deal with her insanity until the baby was born. He needed to know if it was his. If it was, he was going to be a damn good dad, even if that meant saving all the crazy voicemails and texts from Ellen and using them to gain custody of the baby.

He sighed. That would be crazy, wouldn't it? A firefighter who worked twenty-four on and forty-eight off requesting full custody? His family would help out, but... Would he have a chance? Would a judge say 'your schedule is better than her crazy'?

Yeah, his brain was all over the place. He needed to work out, and his two Irish wolfhounds, Oden and Thor, would love a run. So, he started his truck and drove the five miles to his apartment.

Gage, his nephew, lived in the apartment above him and took care of the dogs when Blay was working. The kid wanted a dog desperately, so taking care of his two goofs was a learning experience. He paid Gage to walk them to the park, also known as a rehabbed vacant lot located across the street. He and his brother Brody had purchased the land and fenced it in. Gage was in sight of his parents, and the dogs would eat anyone who tried to mess with the kid. They were loyal and protective and big enough to scare off anyone.

He pulled into his parking space and looked up. Thor and Oden's noses were smushed against the window. He smiled and felt the tension start to leave his shoulders. An avalanche of fur, slobber, and wagging tails met him at the door. The dogs stood on their back feet and were as tall as he was, so the face washing he got every time he returned from a shift had become a ritual. He gave them the attention they needed and deserved before he changed into shorts, a t-shirt, and running shoes.

He took the dogs across the street and let them play and sniff around while he warmed up and stretched. When he was ready, he whistled for the dogs and put their leashes back on. They ran on his left, side by side. Together, the three of them took up the entire sidewalk, and it had been dicey training them to run at his side and not cross in front of him. He swore for the first month the dogs were going to kill him or cripple him, but they'd finally found a method that worked.

He fell into his stride with his dogs loping alongside. They completed the first two-mile loop. The dogs were still crazy with energy, so he pushed out another two miles. He was dead tired, but his dogs needed the exercise, and he needed the quiet the exercise provided. Focusing on his pace and where he and the dogs were was an all-encompassing effort. There wasn't any time to worry about Ellen, Dawn, or his studies for his promotion testing. He simply ran, in the moment, with two animals that loved him and trusted him completely.

By the time they made it back to the apartment, Thor and Oden's tongues were hanging out. They jogged up to his apartment, and he unlocked the door, letting the animals in. After he'd made sure they had water and food, he picked up his phone. No new calls from Ellen. It was almost as if she knew when he was off duty. She rarely called him then, but while he was at work and couldn't answer her calls, the woman went off the rails.

He glanced at the clock. It was late enough. He hit Dawn's number and waited for the phone to connect.

"Hello, handsome. How was the shift?"

Dawn's husky voice hit him like a jolt of electricity; the hovering exhaustion cleared momentarily. "It was a busy one. Apartment fire was the last call." He didn't try to hide the emotion in his voice.

Her sexy voice rose in volume, "Oh, man. Did someone get hurt? Is your crew okay?"

"Everyone from the station is fine, but we lost one that Royal pulled out—a woman. She didn't make it. I brought down a kid we found with her, and another search team found a person in the apartment across the hall. Unfortunately, there was no status update by the time we left, so, for now, they're alive." He ran his hand through his sweaty hair.

"Blay, I'm so sorry. What can I do?"

"Meet me for lunch?"

"I've got a better idea. Come over, and we'll make lunch here and chill. Gage will be here for the day; he and Johnny want to play. We'll play some catch and grill some burgers or something. Bring the monsters with you."

He laughed and looked over at his dogs, who were currently crashed under the window on their dog beds. "Sounds like a plan."

"I still have some dog food here, so we can go to your mom's together in the morning."

"Did she rope you into helping, too?"

"I'll have you know it is a sacred Girl's Night invitation. I'm honored to be used and abused, unlike the other women who do this on the regular."

KRIS MICHAELS

"What does Hover Mother have you doing?"

"First, we are spray painting vases and planters to match. Then we have to assemble the centerpieces and come up with an arrangement of silk flowers that we can add real flowers to."

Blay's curiosity got the better of him. "Ah... why would you want to mix fake and real flowers?"

"How many weddings have you been to?"

"Ah, not many."

"Well, the silk flowers are cheaper than the real ones. But if you build out a nice base and tuck in a few buds and cheap greens, it looks fabulous, and it is done on a budget. Brie has a set amount she's willing to spend for flowers, and she refuses to go over that limit."

He rolled his eyes. "She's marrying into a rich family."

"But Ryker isn't rich, and Brie is living within their budget. I think she's a rock star for sticking to her guns."

Blay's phone sounded, announcing another call. He pulled back the phone and looked at the screen. Ellen. Again.

"Hey, I've got another call coming in. I'll see you in about an hour."

"Don't forget your toothbrush." Dawn's sexy

laughter before she hung up went straight to his balls.

He flicked the screen and answered the call. "What do you need, Ellen?"

"That's a fine way to speak to the mother of your child."

"Presumably." It wasn't a finished deal as far as he was concerned.

"It's yours. I only slept with you."

That was not what the word was on the street, but he couldn't discount her version, so instead, he countered, "So, prove it. I was reading that the child's DNA can be determined by doing a blood test on you. They said you needed to wait eight weeks, but according to you, you're almost four months pregnant now, so it's safe."

Ellen didn't respond for several moments. "Why are you so sure I'm wrong? I know who I slept with, and it was you. Only you."

"Then you shouldn't mind proving I'm the father."

"Why is there a rush? Do you have something going on the side, Blay?"

He snorted. "On the side? That assumes *we* have something. We don't."

Her angry gasp on the other end jerked his head back. "We have a family. We will always have something together. You need to stop seeing whatever skanky bitch you're hooking up with right now!"

Blay pulled the phone from his ear and stared at it for a moment. "First, you have no say in my life, and if you recall, you threw me out of your apartment the minute I said I wanted a paternity test. I haven't initiated contact with you since. You *are not* in my life. Second, you adamantly refuse to do a paternity test, so why would I believe this child is mine? And third, *if* we have a child together and *if* he or she is mine, I'm going to want full custody."

"You have no right to see another woman or to threaten me. I'll show you. You shouldn't make me mad, Blay. I'll show you!" She let off with a string of obscenities that would make his older brothers blush, and that was saying something. Blay made sure the phone was disconnected and stared at the face of it as he tried to sort through all the levels of wrong Ellen's outraged rant bubbled to the surface.

Oden padded over and dropped his head on Blay's shoulder. He reached up and stroked the dog's wiry hair. Oden was the comforter of the two; Thor, the protector. "Yeah, I know, boy. The woman's crazy." He stood up and continued to rub the dog's scruff. "I probably need to look into hiring a lawyer."

Thor lifted his head and growled. There was a

knock at the door a second later. Blay made his way to the door and, out of habit, looked out the peephole. He smiled and opened the door for his brother, Brody.

"Hiding from the family?"

Brody rolled his eyes and pushed past him. "No. Do you know what type of arch Mom wants for Brie's wedding? I was thinking of a simple frame, and they'd decorate it, you know? But no, she wants it square with an arched walk-through. Then, when the wedding is over, she wants it moved to the gate so she can plant climbing roses around it. We aren't talking a day's worth of beer-in-hand construction here, Blay. She wants Homes and Gardens type shit." Brody dropped to the couch. "Get a piece of paper. We need to figure this out."

"Can't. I'm taking a shower and then going over to Dawn's."

"Amber is heading there now to drop off Gage." Brody rubbed his chin before his head popped up. "Why are you going to Dawn's?"

Blay cocked his head at his brother. "Why do you think?"

Brody's eyes grew huge. "No way."

"Dude, you sounded thirteen just now." Blay

pulled off his shirt and headed into his bedroom and the best bachelor bathroom ever built.

"I do not, and since when?" Brody followed him along with Thor and Oden.

Oh great, an audience. Well, it didn't bother him to get naked in front of his dogs or his brother. He shucked his shorts and briefs then lobbed them into the laundry basket before he opened the door to the massive multi-head shower he'd installed. "I don't know, maybe four months or so."

"And I'm just now finding out about this?"

Brody's voice rose higher, and Blay shot him a look before he stepped in the shower. "Not my fault you don't talk to your wife."

"Amber knows?" Brody turned and looked at the dogs. "Did *you two* know?"

Thor sat down, and Oden licked his arm. "Figured." He swung his attention back to Blay. "You know you can't screw this up, right? That's Gage's aunt, and we invite her to all the family gatherings. Didn't you think this through? I can see epic messes, which means Hover Mother will be in the middle of it."

"Dude, do you hear yourself right now?" Blay soaped up while he stared at his brother.

"What?" Brody lifted his arms.

"You sound like Mom."

His brother dropped his arms and glared at him. "That was uncalled for and a seriously low blow."

Blay chuckled and turned his back on Brody. "Whatever, man. It isn't your business, so keep your nose out of it."

He washed his hair before he turned around. Brody and the dogs were still there. "You know, I bought this apartment from you so I could take a shower without an audience."

"Get over yourself. I'll take a breather on the Dawn issue, but you have to help me with the design of that damn arch before you leave. Thirty minutes. That's all."

Blay sighed and turned off the shower. "Thirty minutes, not a second more."

CHAPTER 2

D awn watched her sister pull up into the driveway from the gate by the backyard. "Hey, over here." She waved and saw her nephew wave back from the passenger seat. Both he and his mom got out of the small SUV and walked across the grass. "You're right on time. I could use some help." She opened the gate and waved at the pavers she wanted to put down to form a walk to the back-yard. She'd already spent two weekends leveling the ground, so putting the pavers in place should be a cinch.

"Why did you dig it up?" Gage asked and walked over to the pavers, picking one up. "These are heavy."

"Well, I leveled it. I thought we could lay the bricks down and get some sand between the pavers before we grilled up some lunch." Dawn closed the gate behind Amber.

"We can help." Amber dropped her keys into her purse. "Take this inside, buddy, and then come back out to help."

"Okay, can I get a pop?"

Answering at the same time, they both automatically spit out opposite answers, "Sure," coming from Dawn while Amber replied, "No."

Gage smiled. "Aunt Dawn's house, her rules." The boy bolted around the corner and into the house.

"You're spoiling him." Amber grabbed two pavers.

"Always. Because I can send him home to you and Brody. Speaking of which, weren't you going to go home and spend some time with him?" She lifted her eyebrows a couple of times. "You can't be tired of each other already."

Amber snorted. "Hardly, but he's going to recruit Blay to help him get a head start on that wedding arch. From the way he's been whining all morning, Hannah has changed it from a simple premise to a small construction job that could take a while to complete."

"Blay?" Dawn snugged the first paver into its place and reached back for the next one.

"Yeah, why? Did you guys have something planned?"

"I thought we did. We just talked not more than a half-hour ago." She laid the other paver and then put a level between the two stones. Next, she tapped on the right side of one of the stones using a rubber mallet until it was level.

"Brody was going to go downstairs after he finished talking to his new captain, so depending on how long that took, it could be he hadn't been recruited when he talked to you."

Dawn's cell phone dinged, and she pulled it out from her back pocket. She glanced at the text.

>*Brody's being a PITA. Be there ASAP. P.S. He knows.*

She snorted and replied back.

>*About time. Bad detective.*

Glancing up at Amber, she accepted another paver and dropped it into its place. "Looks like Brody finally knows about Blay and me."

"The guy is oblivious to what happens in the

family. He's damn good at picking up the smallest details at work, but at home, it is almost as if he has blinders on." Amber handed her another paver.

She set it down and went through the leveling process, placing the new stones and then placing the level between the new and old stones to make sure they were perfect.

Gage strolled back with a soda in his hand. "That's cool." He pointed to the diamond shapes the pavers were making.

"And it's easy. Come here, and I'll show you how to do it." Dawn motioned down to where she was on her hands and knees. Gage came beside her and settled down on his knees, too. "Now, we place the next one like this."

Gage followed her instructions for the next stone. They worked together till they finished the path down the side of the house.

Amber dusted off her hands and pulled her phone from the back pocket of her shorts. She shook her head. "Seems like Brody has kidnapped Blay. They're going to the lumber yard before they swing back to get the dogs. They'll all be here in a couple hours." Amber glanced down at her. "Sorry, I think my husband hijacked your boyfriend."

Gage's head popped up. "Blay is your boyfriend?"

Dawn blinked in surprise. "Ahh… we're dating, yes." She set the level on the last stone.

Gage sat on his heels. "Are you dating other guys?"

Dawn tapped the stone down into the earth. "Well, no."

"Does he know you're dating?"

Dawn sat back on her heels and laughed. "Yes, I'm positive he knows we're dating."

"Then he's your boyfriend. Cool. But you can't ever do what Stacy Lawson did." Gage sprang up and grabbed his soda, taking a swig.

Amber asked, "What did Stacy do this time?" She looked over at Dawn. "A new girl at school. I hear about her a lot."

Gage grunted and then exploded, "She told the whole school she and Finn were boyfriend and girlfriend, but she didn't tell Finn. That's not right. He should get to say if they are, shouldn't he?"

Dawn nodded, suddenly serious because her nephew was asking her a more profound question than he realized. "Absolutely. Both people should agree to the relationship. If one side says no, the answer is no. Right?"

Gage nodded. "Yeah, Dad says if anyone says no, you gotta respect that. But Stacy didn't give Finn the chance to say no. She's bossy. Worse than Grandma when she gets going."

Dawn tried for about five seconds to hold back the laugh. Hannah had a heart of gold, but the woman was a human tornado at times.

"Gage, we don't talk about Grandma that way." Amber's reprimand would have held more weight if she hadn't been laughing so hard.

Gage made a face. "Dad does, so does Uncle Brock and Uncle Blay and Aunt—"

"Okay, we get it." Amber dropped a hand on his shoulder.

Dawn stood up and brushed off her knees. "Well, I'm going to pop into the shower since we have time, and then how about we make some hamburgers and stuff them with cheese?"

"Yay! My favorite." Gage pumped the air with his fist. "Can I go across the street and see if Johnny is home?" He turned to look at his mom, so Dawn kept her mouth shut this time.

"Sure, but come back when you see your dad's truck." Amber's words were shouted at Gage's back because the kid was already down the pathway they'd just put into place. Amber grimaced and looked at her. "Did he mess up the stones?"

"Nah, that ground is compacted. Blay and I

leveled it, and he's run a weighted barrel over it. I'll pour the pea gravel in the cracks later." They walked to the back of the house and entered the kitchen.

"Listen, we didn't mean to invade your time with Blay. Brody, Gage, and I can leave."

Dawn snorted. "Like you could haul Brody out of here. You know how he is. He's going to want all the details, and then he'll want to be the one to bless the arrangement."

Amber chuckled. "He will, but he means it in the best possible way."

"You deal with your husband when he shows up, and I'll be happy. I'm going to wash off. I'll be right back. Make yourself at home." Dawn laughed as she walked down the hall. Amber and Gage had lived with her for ten years. This was as much Amber's home as hers.

She closed her bedroom door behind her and stripped out of her dirty cutoffs and tank top. Piling her shoulder-length brown hair up on top of her head in a messy bun, she took a quick shower and changed into a pair of new shorts and a cute summer top that she'd seen online and had to have. She slipped into her sandals and headed to the kitchen.

Amber already had the potatoes on the stove boiling

for the salad. She opened the fridge and retrieved the celery, onions, bell peppers, and hard-boiled eggs. "How's work going?" she asked Amber as she sat the items on the counter. They both grabbed knives and shared the large cutting board, working in a way only ten years of cooking in the same kitchen could form.

"We had a huge bust last week—over a million in prescription drugs. Rayburn and Watson were voluntold to run down the lot numbers. You ought to hear those two idiots arguing. It was weird not having Ryker at the helm, but the new captain is good, and although he runs things differently, he gives us high cover." Amber tossed a bite of celery into her mouth. "What about you? How're things?"

Dawn reached over and grabbed the onion. As she sliced it, she answered, "I'm going to have to do a mass hatchet job next week. We have three people who are messing up by the numbers and they work in the same section, so the section chief isn't doing his job. We've had shipments screwed ten ways to Sunday. When one vendor calls and complains, okay, it could be a fluke. We talk to the driver, and then we check the manifest to make sure the vendor actually ordered what he says he did. When seven vendors call, it's us. Warehousing is going to get a clean sweep. Clyde is going to train the new section chief himself."

Amber scrunched her nose. "When the owner is on the floor, you know you have issues."

"That section chief was just promoted. My gut told me he wasn't the one for the job. I told Clyde that, too." She shook her head. "He told me training the new guy was his penance for not listening to me."

"Clyde would be lost without you." Amber moved to the sink to peel the hardboiled eggs.

"Nah, but I do make his life easier. That company has grown since I started. Did you know we're now the third largest distribution center in the state? When I started, he had thirty trucks and was renting distribution space. Now he has more warehouses than you can shake a stick at and over 300 rigs."

"How much is that man worth?"

Amber sat an egg on the board, and she sliced it up as she answered, "I don't really know. Thank God I'm only the office manager."

Amber barked out a laugh. "That may be your job description, but you know you're Clyde's right hand."

Dawn chuckled along with her. "True, he actually gave me a pay raise a while back."

"What? Congratulations. Did he say why?"

Dawn gave her sister a conspiratorial grin. "I may have been looking for jobs that paid better, and word got back to him. I knew with you gone I'd need to make a bit more so I could still save and invest in my IRAs. He asked me what it would take to get me to stay, and I told him. He didn't even blink. He just said, 'Done.'"

Amber's jaw went slack. "How much did you ask for?"

"Double."

"No way. Shut the front door!"

"Way."

"Oh my God, Dawn, that is amazing!"

"I know, right? But believe me, I'm earning every last dollar. Clyde just bought out Keller Transportation. That's where the new guy and the crew in warehousing came from."

"Keller Transportation, the one with the property down by the harbor? A couple of good warehouses and then a lot of empty ones in disrepair?"

Dawn paused her slicing and looked up at her sister. "You have that tone in your voice."

"What tone?" Amber blinked at her in confusion.

"Your DEA tone. Why do you know where Keller Transportation is?"

"Ah, well, let's just say the location has come up in a couple of our investigations."

Dawn dropped the knife on the cutting board. "No. For the love of my sanity, tell me that you are not investigating Keller Transportation."

Amber wagged her head a bit before she answered, "Not exactly investigating."

Dawn put her hand on her hip. "Meaning?"

"Meaning when did Clyde finish the purchase?"

"Last month on the tenth."

"Huh. So, do you think Rayburn, Watson, and I could get an appointment with Clyde next week?"

"Ah, crud, Amber." Dawn dropped her head back and stared at the ceiling. "He didn't do anything wrong; he just bought the darn company."

"No, no, we aren't looking at the owner, but since I *do* have an in with the *new* owner, maybe we can put a person in the warehouse and chase down a few leads. But that goes no further, understand? You can't discuss this with anyone."

Dawn shook her head. "You're using me for work?"

"Of course! If I can't use my sister, who can I use?" Amber popped another piece of celery into her mouth and crunched it.

"Well, damn it, if you're going to make sense, I'm

going to stop talking to you." Dawn moved across the kitchen to grab a bowl to mix the ingredients for the potato salad.

"No, don't stop. You have to dish on you and Blay." Amber lifted herself onto the counter and grabbed a celery stick, taking a bite out of it.

"Dish?" Dawn stopped and looked at her. "Since when do I dish on my dates?"

Amber spread her hands wide, "Since forever! Oh, check the potatoes. They should be ready."

Dawn picked up a fork and speared one of the baby Yukon golds. "Nope, not quite yet."

"So?" Amber stretched the word out.

"What do you want to know?" Dawn went to the fridge and pulled out two light beers. She popped the top on one and gave it to Amber, then popped the top on hers.

"The usual," Amber spoke slowly as if she was talking to a simpleton.

Dawn took a sip of her beer and then drew a deep breath. "Well, he's hell on wheels in the sack."

"It must run in the family." Amber clapped her hands together. "I'm so happy for you, but how is the relationship going? It's not all about sex, you know."

Dawn snorted. "Really? I hadn't figured that out."

Amber chucked a piece of celery at her. "Stop being obtuse; answer me."

Dawn picked up the stray veggie and tossed it into the sink. "I like him, Amber. I mean, I really like him. We've been dating for four months, and we're going slow. Well, except for the sex. I like it hard and fast."

Amber choked on the beer she was drinking. "Oh, my God! You timed that!"

Dawn laughed and shrugged. "Serves you right for throwing food."

"The potatoes are boiling over." Amber slid off the counter and went to the cupboard for a strainer while she turned off the pot and strained the contents.

Dawn grabbed a cookie sheet and Amber rolled the potatoes out on it to help them cool quicker. "Seriously, though, I'm happy. He has a lot of stress and pressure on the job, so we tend to stick to the lighter topics. I like to make him laugh." Dawn stared out the window. "He's so serious all the time. It's like he's got this weight on his shoulders."

"I can imagine. Sean told Brody the apartment complex fire they responded to last night had three fatalities." Amber pulled the hamburger out of the refrigerator.

"Three? Oh, damn, he doesn't know that. He said the woman died, but the child he brought out and another victim were still alive." She knew how hard this would hit him. Maybe they could go for a run after Brody, Amber, and Gage left. But then again, if they were going to have a backyard barbeque, maybe the topic wouldn't come up. But keeping it from him would be wrong too.

"Hey, where did you go?"

Amber, closer than she remembered, startled her. "Oh, sorry. Just thinking."

"About Blay? He sure is handsome." Amber hip-checked her on the way to the counter with cheese. *Huh, I really must have zoned out.*

Dawn went to the spice rack and pulled out their favorites. "Does your husband know you think his little brother is handsome?"

Amber snorted. "All the King men are freaking gorgeous, and you know it."

Dawn chuckled and sprinkled seasoning into the ground meat. Blay was beyond handsome, in her opinion. He'd received his mother's darker hair, and his eyes were a light blue. His body was chiseled perfection. Seriously, the ridges on the man were a sensual playground that she used as often as she could. But it wasn't just about the sex. Blay was fun and had the same interests as she did. They both loved old rock and roll. The eighties had epic love ballads that played on a loop when they made love. He loved animals, and his dogs were sweet and protective, just like him. Dawn snorted out a laugh, and her sister looked at her.

"What?"

"I kinda compared Blay to his dogs in my mind. You know, protective and sweet."

Amber's laugh echoed through the kitchen. "Is he sweet?"

Dawn stiffened. "Amber, don't you dare tease him."

Her sister held up her hands. "Nope. I'd never embarrass you that way. I promise."

"Okay." Dawn let a smile grow across her face. "He is the most romantic man I've ever dated."

"Blay?" Amber gawked at her. Her mouth hung open. "Blay, the one his brothers called a manwhore?"

"Stop. That was before." Or so Dawn told herself. She'd heard all the rumors, and when she'd gone to the Celtic Cock with Kallie and Amber, she'd seen how many of the women circled Blay and his crew. "Besides, we aren't exclusive."

"Well, why the hell not?" Amber asked as they

formed patties and put indentions in the middle to hold the shredded cheese.

"Because he hasn't brought it up." Dawn grabbed a handful of ground meat.

Amber took another scoop of meat. "You know, in this day and age, the woman can offer input into the relationship. He doesn't have to mention it. You could."

Dawn rolled her eyes. "Really? You don't say?"

Amber hip-checked her again, causing her to take two steps to the side. "Stop. If you think this is a relationship you want to grow, ask him for exclusivity."

She shrugged. "I'll think about it. But, as I said, I'm happy with what we have now."

Amber nodded and put the last patty on the platter. "Gotcha, but ask yourself: if Blay goes out to the Cock and some young, pretty firefighter groupie flirts with him, how would you feel?"

Dawn walked to the sink to wash her hands. How would she feel about it? Well, she sure as hell wouldn't be happy. She looked over her shoulder at Amber. "How would being exclusive change that scenario?"

"He'd come home to you, not go somewhere with

her." Amber took a butcher knife and carefully cut the potatoes in half.

Dawn put the stopper in the drain and started the water to wash the cookware they'd used so far. "Don't you think it's too soon to talk about that? I don't want to come across as needy."

"Girl, you are the most self-sufficient person on this planet. If Blay can't see that, then he is brain-damaged. You've been dating for four months. Sleeping together for…" Amber lifted her eyebrows in question.

Dawn let a smile creep across her face. "Four months."

Amber laughed, "You easy thing!"

"Ha! He'd been asking me out for months. I wasn't easy. But damn, the sex is phenomenal." Dawn laughed. "He lifts me like I weigh nothing, and I love how I feel next to him, and yet I never feel like I'm in his shadow, you know? I can just be myself with him and relax, knowing he sees me for me."

Amber smiled at her from across the kitchen. "I know exactly what you mean. It's called love, and it is the most wonderful thing in the world."

Dawn turned off the water in the sink and shook her head. "It can't be love. Not this soon. We aren't shifters."

Amber swallowed a drink of her beer. "Excuse me? What? You aren't what?"

Dawn lifted a hand out of the sudsy water and waved it. "Never mind." She'd explain her latest reading binge later.

Amber let it go but continued, "Whatever. Love doesn't run on a timetable, Dawn. If it did, Brody and I would be so screwed." Amber took another drink of her beer. That would most certainly be true. They'd wasted ten years of their lives before they finally figured it out.

She washed and rinsed the things they'd used while they visited about Gage's school. When they'd stuffed the burgers and put them back into the fridge, they moved the conversation to the back porch.

"What time are you going to be at Blay's mom and dad's?" Dawn adjusted the umbrella so they were both in the shade.

"Brody wants to get there early. I think I'll let him and Gage go when the sun rises. I need to clean and do laundry before I go over. Why? When are you going over?"

"I'm riding over with Blay."

"You realize Hannah will notice, right?"

Dawn shrugged. "She'll find out anyway. Gage tells her everything."

Amber lifted her beer and agreed, "Gage is her information conduit. Here's to your health. May you survive the Hover Mother interrogation."

CHAPTER 3

Blay pulled into Dawn's driveway and sent a side-eyed stare at his brother. Thirty minutes had turned into three hours. He should have left his brother hanging. Should have said no and come over to help Dawn. If she laid the stones, he'd spread the gravel between the rocks to finish the pathway. They'd been working on the small things in her home—things he could teach her how to do. The larger things he'd rather she let him do, but she'd been very adamant that she wasn't lazy and could be taught.

He, Brody, and the dogs found the women in the backyard. Amber greeted Brody with a kiss, and for the first time around his family, Dawn came into his arms and gave him a kiss. And damn, what a kiss it was. He tightened his hold on her and returned the kiss with enthusiasm.

"Okay, okay, my son is supposed to be here somewhere. Keep it P.G., will you?" Brody admonished them.

He lifted away and stared into her beautiful hazel-green eyes. "Hey, you."

She wound her fingers through the hair at the back of his neck. "Hey."

"Hi, Brody, how are you? I'm fine, thank you, Dawn. It's great to see you again. I know, it's been so long," Brody mimicked the conversation.

Dawn leaned to the left and chastised her brother-in-law, "Stop whining and go get yourself a beer."

Brody smiled widely. "That's even better. You want one, Blay?"

"No, thanks. I didn't get any sleep last night, and I'll end up snoring in the sun if I drink."

"Long night?" Amber asked.

"Very. Three callouts. It seemed like we'd clear one and be just falling asleep when the klaxon would sound again." Dawn motioned to the chair, and he sat down, pulling her onto his lap with him.

Brody exited with the beers. "What are we talking about?"

"Blay's last shift." Amber filled him in.

"Yeah, Sean said that the last one was a bad one." He sat down beside Amber and took her hand.

Dawn leaned into Blay and relaxed until Oden trotted up and licked her foot. She giggled and scratched his ears. "I'll go get them some water and put out their food."

She called to them, and they both trotted after her.

"When did you talk to Sean?"

"This morning. I had to meet an informant, and on the way back, I stopped at the diner to bring home breakfast. Sean was there."

Blay yawned. "Did he say what started it?"

Brody took a swig of his beer and shook his head. "You know him; he won't say anything official until all the evidence is processed. But, off the record, it looks like it could be arson." He shook his head. "I couldn't do what you do. I couldn't go into those flames."

Blay shrugged. "I couldn't do what you do. Fire is predictable. People aren't."

Brody nodded and was about to say something when Gage tore through the side gate. "Dad!" The boy flew across the yard like a heat-seeking rocket. Brody had just enough time to hand off his beer before Gage jumped on him. "Hey, big man. What have you been up to?"

"Playing with Johnny. He has a new football. Can you and Uncle Blay play catch with us?"

Brody glanced at him. He smiled and nodded. If he didn't get his ass out of the chair, he'd be falling asleep. "We can play keep away from the dogs. They need some more exercise."

"Cool! Be right back." Gage tore off at full tilt.

"Be careful!"

"Look before you cross!" Amber and Brody called at the same time.

Gage's "Yeah, yeah," was followed by the gate slamming.

Four hours later, Blay dropped his arm over Dawn's shoulders as Brody, Gage, and Amber pulled out of the driveway in her vehicle. "Sorry about not getting here sooner. I wanted to help with the walkway. It looks great, by the way." He pulled her into a hug and held her close.

She sighed and leaned into his embrace. "Call me silly, but I like the fact we didn't have to behave in front of them."

"Behave?" Blay loosened his grip so she could look up.

"You know. We were able to hold hands, hug, kiss. I didn't realize how much that bothered me until today. Not touching you."

He smiled down at her. "I never asked you not to do that."

She closed one eye and squinted the other. He'd seen that expression before. It was her 'I want to disagree with you but not argue about it' look. "Spill it."

She made a slight grimace. "You kinda did."

He blinked and searched his mind for how he managed that feat. He came up with nothing. "How?"

"By not introducing me to your mother and father as someone you're dating the next time we were both at their house." She shrugged as if it didn't mean anything.

He held her at arm's length and looked her in the eye. "I thought I was doing the right thing. I didn't want you to deal with the flack everyone in my family would shoot off if we didn't last."

She nodded. "I get that. But we've lasted. Brody knows."

"And Gage, so Mom will know within minutes of him getting there tomorrow."

Dawn chuckled, "True. So, I'm going to ask something."

He cocked his head. "You say that with a bit of trepidation."

"Yeah, so here it goes. Can we be exclusive?" She didn't look at him when she asked. When he didn't answer, she lifted her eyes to him and then lifted her eyebrows. "What?"

He closed his eyes and sighed. "Let's go sit down. I need to let you know about a situation before we take that next step."

She narrowed her eyes. "How bad? Am I going to need a glass of wine?"

He motioned to the couch. "I'll get the wine."

"Shit." She turned and walked into the front room. "You're scaring me here, King."

"I don't mean to. Just give me a second." He grabbed a glass from the cupboard and poured her a glass of chardonnay that she had open in the refrigerator and was back and sitting down beside her seconds later. "I don't know how to tell you this, so I'm just going to spit it out."

Dawn leaned forward. "Go ahead."

"Before I met you, there was this woman. I spent two nights with her. Hell, Dawn, this sounds horrible, but I barely remember her." He wiped his palms against his shorts. "She, ah... claims that I'm the father of her baby."

Dawn stared at him for a couple of long moments before she broke eye contact and reached for her wine. He sat silent as she drank the wine and placed the glass back on the coffee table. "Paternity test?"

"I asked for one. She threw me out of her apartment upstate when I did. Since then, I've hired a private investigator, who confirmed she was pregnant."

"Do you think the baby is yours?"

"No. I'm meticulous, Dawn. I suited up, and I checked the condom after."

"Condoms aren't a hundred percent." She reached for her wine glass again.

"I know. That's why I want a paternity test. Look, this woman is crazy." He pulled out his cell phone and opened the voicemail app. "Scroll down. That's her number. Listen to any or all of them. I'm telling you, she's not right, and I think she's trying to play me. I took her to my apartment. She's seen where I live and knows I have nice things."

"Because you busted your ass." Dawn snarked. He'd walked her through his apartment and shown her what he and Brody had built.

"Yeah, but she doesn't know that. She's a chippy that hangs around firefighters. I'm honest when I tell you I don't think that baby is mine."

Dawn scrolled and scrolled and scrolled. She handed the phone back. "So, what are you going to do?"

He sighed. "I'm going to demand a paternity test and keep demanding it. Right now, all she is is a nuisance."

"And if the baby is yours?" She lifted her eyes to him and stared at him.

He held his phone a bit. "If it is mine, I'll step up to the plate. Also, I'm considering using this crazy and all the rest of the texts and voice messages to file for sole custody. I don't want a son or daughter of mine to grow up around that."

Dawn drew a deep breath and then nodded. "Okay."

Blay jolted. "Okay? What's that mean?"

Dawn lifted her glass again and took another drink. "There's always baggage in a relationship. This is yours. Okay."

Blay rubbed his face. "Dawn, sweetheart, I'm beyond exhausted, and my brain isn't firing on all eight cylinders. What does that mean?"

"It means that I understand that you and this

woman were together before we started to date. Okay, you have a past, but so do I. So, I'm not judging you. Does it surprise me that you have a maybe baby momma? Yes. I mean, who wouldn't be shocked? This is a hell of a big deal. But I'm not going to let her stop me from being happy."

He stared at her, still not connecting any dots she had strung together with those words. He leaned forward and dropped his elbows onto his knees. "Dawn, does that mean you still want to go out with me, or does that mean you're kicking me to the curb?"

She snorted out a laugh. "Damn, handsome, you are tired, aren't you?" She slid over and kissed him. "It means I'm willing to take it a day at a time and deal with whatever happens in... Wait, how pregnant is she?"

Blay took her hand in his. "Just over four months."

"Okay. We'll deal with what happens in five months or so. Who knows what the future holds?"

He tugged her onto his lap. "Do you still want to be exclusive? And for the record, I haven't been with anyone else since you said yes."

She straddled him and leaned down, staring at him. "Yes, but we are both going to get tested and show each other the results. You have a reputation, and I'm not going to lie; I have had a few dates that were one and done."

He slid his hands up to her waist and then down, cupping her ass. "I'll go the next weekday I have off, and I'll introduce you as my girlfriend tomorrow."

Dawn chuckled. "If we beat Gage there, you mean?"

"There is that," he conceded.

"Go take the monsters out for the night. I'll make sure they have food and water. Then come to bed. You're exhausted."

He caught her before she could stand. "I'm not that exhausted." He kissed her, sweeping her lips with his tongue. She opened for him, and he devoured her. Turning, he moved her onto the couch. He moved over her and settled between her long legs which she wrapped around him. He pressed against her core, still clothed, but damn, the noise she made drove him wild.

His hand went to the button of her shorts. She grabbed his wrist and broke the kiss. "The drapes are open, and the dogs need to go out. Go, and we'll finish this in bed."

He stared at her kiss swollen lips and dipped for

another kiss, then another. Finally, she laughed, "Stop. Now. Go take care of your animals."

"I'm trying!" Blay laughed and dropped his forehead to her shoulder.

"Poor baby." She ran her fingers through his hair.

"You have no idea." His balls were probably a royal shade of blue right now. He lifted up and carefully stood, offering her a hand up. She slid up to him and slid a hand against his cock. The feel of the material between them as she stroked was frustrating and fantastic and fucking evil. He groaned and spun away. Her laughter followed him and the dogs out the door. He let the dogs do their business, cleaned up after them, and then went into the guest bathroom to wash up. He opened Dawn's bedroom door after telling the dogs to stay. They dropped to their haunches and stared at him. He shut the door behind him without a twinge of remorse. They were spoiled, and not being able to be in the room while he and Dawn were busy wasn't going to hurt them.

"Hello, handsome."

He turned and about swallowed his tongue. Dawn was wearing a yellow teddy that fit her runner's body like a glove. The lace and material covered while it teased, and damn, he didn't need any teasing to get interested. He locked his eyes on her and slowly crossed the room. "It's not going to be slow tonight." He trailed a finger down her arm, and gooseflesh followed in its wake.

Dawn lifted a chin. "Who said I wanted it slow?"

"Get on the bed. Hands and knees." He tossed off his shirt as he toed off his shoes. His shorts, briefs, and socks were gone just as quickly.

She was on her hands and knees, looking back at him, her mouth partially open, and the flush to her skin was rose-colored and sexy as fuck. She was as hungry for him as he was for her.

It was an anomaly for him. Repeat performances got old quickly in his book. But not with Dawn. With her, he wanted to take the time to get to know her, know her body and know what made her explode. Not tonight. He stroked his shaft and shuddered as his cock bucked in his hand. He reached to the nightstand and retrieved the box of condoms he'd put there. He suited up his stiff-as-fuck cock and leaned down, moving her thick fall of brown hair, kissing her on the back of the neck. He trailed those kisses down the yellow lace to the dimples at her back. When he got there, he ran a finger under the lace to the snaps that held the garment together at the crotch. In the work of a second, he popped the clasps free and continued his trail of kisses. Over her tight ass, he trailed his tongue and bit before he kissed the sting away. He reached up and pushed her down. She went to her chest, and he wrapped his arms around her hips, pulling her up so he could taste her. He didn't give her warning but dove in, delving into her depths. She pushed back against him, and he doubled his efforts.

Her body was writhing under his tongue and lips. Dawn wasn't quiet in bed, and she wasn't a passive participant. Her words of encouragement or direction were muffled against the bed, but he got the idea. He found her clit and rubbed the little nub as he feasted. It didn't take long for her to reach her climax. He lapped and kissed until she went limp. Then he kneeled behind her, found her core, and slid home.

They both groaned at the same time. Blay nudged her, and she dropped to the bed. He wrapped his arms under hers, and they kissed in a sideways, messy, languid kiss that lasted forever and ended too soon when he broke the kiss to adjust and breathe.

As much as he wanted to make the night last, he was going to come too soon for her to reach another climax. He lifted his hips and drove into her, setting a fast tempo that sent strobing surges of electricity through him, pooling at the base of his spine. He leaned down and gently bit her shoulder as he plunged deeper and deeper. She braced herself against the headboard, and he closed his eyes, letting go. The sound of sex filled the room, then his shout chased those sounds. Red exploded through the black of his closed eyes. His body, on automatic, pumped into her like a jackhammer. He slowed and only then remembered to breathe. He filled his chest with air and blew it out. "Oh, damn, that was fucking fantastic." He breathed the words against her bare shoulder.

She nodded and patted his hair. Breathless and panting, she agreed, "Yeah, fucking fantastic."

Blay pulled out carefully and sat up on his heels. He needed to take care of the condom, but damn it, he didn't have the energy. He looked down and blinked at what he saw.

The condom had broken.

"Oh, fuck."

Dawn popped up on her elbows and looked back. "What?"

He rolled off the condom and held up the useless piece of latex. "I…" He lifted his eyes to hers. "Please, tell me you are on birth control."

Dawn twisted, moving her leg to sit up. She stared at the condom and shook her head. "I am. I had an IUD. I had it removed last week, and I just started the pill."

"Is it effective within only a week?" Blay reached for a tissue on the nightstand and wrapped the condom as he spoke.

"I, ah… hold on." Dawn moved to the other side of the bed and her phone. She started tapping on the screen while he padded to the bathroom to dispose of the condom. "Yeah, it says here that it is effective after a week. It has been six days. We should be safe."

"That has never happened to me before. This brand is the best there is." Blay picked up the box and stared at the black and gold box, wishing like hell the damn thing was a punching bag. How could he have not noticed? "I'm sorry."

She pulled the teddy off and dropped it on the floor before slipping between the sheets. "Come to bed. There's nothing we can do about it now."

"Isn't there a morning-after pill you can take?" He lifted the sheets and slid in, pulling her slender body toward his.

She lifted to her elbow and looked down at him. "There is. Don't worry; I'll take care of it. We can meet at your mom's house."

He elbowed up, mimicking her pose. "No, this

isn't on you. I'll go with you, then we can head to the 'rents' house."

She cocked her head and stared at him. "You'd do that? Come with me?"

He pushed her hair from her face and leaned in for a kiss. "I'd do anything you asked me to do. In case you haven't figured it out, I really, really like you."

"Yeah?" She chuckled and smiled at him. "What are we, thirteen?"

"Tonight, we are." Blay pushed her onto her back and leaned over her. "Admit it. You like me, too."

She snaked her arms around his neck. "It was me who asked for an exclusive relationship, right?"

He nodded. "Tell me."

She laughed and shook her head. "Read between the lines, handsome."

"Nope." He pounced on her, his fingers extended. She screeched and started laughing. The dogs started barking. Her squeals kept them barking, but he wasn't going to stop until she admitted it.

"Okay! Okay! I like you, you brute."

He stopped tickling her and stared down at her.

She sobered and lifted her hand to his cheek. "Don't make me regret admitting that."

He slowly scanned the honest vulnerability that

shone in her eyes. He felt the connection that they'd formed. Theirs was more than just a sexual relationship; it was... powerful and consuming. "I will never intentionally hurt you, Dawn."

"I know, that's why taking a step in this direction is so damn scary." Her whisper revealed even more than her admission had.

There were stages past 'like' and before 'love'. They were somewhere in the murky grey waters that spanned that distance. It was a risk. One he was willing to take, and it would seem she would, too. "I'm right there with you. The exact same spot." He leaned down and kissed her.

She sighed and snuggled closer to him. "Go to sleep, handsome. We'll figure it out."

He pulled her closer and took a deep breath, letting go of everything. Tomorrow would bring its own challenges, but tonight, he'd hold the woman that was slowly stealing his heart.

CHAPTER 4

Dawn stared down at the brown paper sack that her purchase sat in. Buying the emergency contraceptive was as easy as a walk down the family planning aisle. It was hanging right beside the condoms. She shook her head and looked out the window of Blay's truck. The dogs panted in the backseat but were content to stick their noses out the small crack in the windows that Blay lowered for them.

"What's wrong?" Blay reached over and took her hand. "You're very quiet, and that's never a good thing."

She laughed and moved the paper bag to the dashboard. "I'm just in a funk. I don't know why I thought getting that pill would be more of a production. I mean, if you think about it, it's kind of wrong. Well, not wrong, but… Ah, hell, I don't know. But, as I said, I'm in a funk."

Blay pulled over and put the truck in park. He took off his seatbelt and turned to her. "Are you doing this for you or me?"

For him. He already had one baby momma. She shook her head, but she'd been with Amber when she went through the pregnancy and delivery. She'd raised Gage with her sister. When they were going through it, she wouldn't have chosen that path. She would have terminated the pregnancy, but her life had changed. Her perspective wasn't that of a young woman just starting her life. She was in a good place now. Did she want to be pregnant? No. Did she want to terminate the pregnancy if she was? She sighed and stared at her fingers. No.

"Hey, talk to me, sweetheart. We're in this together." Blay lifted her chin with a crooked finger.

She met his gaze and sighed again. "When Amber got pregnant and she went through everything, I was there with her. We stayed up at night worried when Gage was sick, I've changed a landfill of diapers, and if you had asked me at that point if I would ever consider having a baby, I would have screamed 'No!'"

Blay tucked a piece of her long brown hair behind her ear. "But now?"

"To be honest, I'm not sure. I can't tell you what my hesitancy is, but..."

"When we read the packaging in the store it said you could take it up to five days after the unprotected sex. So, don't take it today. Think about it. We can talk about it and figure out what the best course for both of us is."

She lifted her chin. "You're really calm about this."

He shrugged. "I've already thought about everything that's going through your mind. I've had almost four months to figure out what I feel is the right thing to do. If Ellen's baby is mine, I'll be a damn good dad. If you decide you don't want to take that pill, I'll do right by you and the baby, too. But the right thing with you will be completely different from what is happening with Ellen. Remember, we're in the same murky waters in this relationship. We're doing something neither of us has done before, and we're navigating these new feelings together. I'm not going to tell you what to do. I'll be here if you take the pill, and I'll be right here if you don't. I only ask that you examine the whys of your hesitancy and make sure they're legitimate and not an emotional knee-jerk reaction."

"Wow." She blinked and then shook her head.

"What?" His brow furrowed tightly.

Dawn smiled. "You're going to make a great dad someday. That was high-level wisdom right there."

Blay snorted a laugh. "I better write it down; I don't get those flashes of greatness often."

"No?" She winked at him.

He leaned forward and kissed her. "The last time was when I asked you out."

She kissed him and then leaned back. "Which time?"

"All four hundred fifty-seven times." Blay strapped his seatbelt back on and hit the turn indicator to merge back into traffic.

She waited until he merged and quipped, "Is that all it was? Seemed like more."

He chuckled and shook his head. "You were a hard sell, but I knew I could wear you down."

She took the pills from the dashboard and put them in her purse, zipping it shut. She would take the time to sort through what was going on in her head. Blay was right; knee-jerk emotional responses weren't a good reason for a decision that ultimately could alter her and his lives forever.

Oden stuck his head over the seat back and was immediately reprimanded. "No, back." Blay had worked to get the dogs to understand they weren't permitted in the front seat. Oden whined a bit but laid back down, dropping his head on Thor's hindquarters. "That's a good boy." Blay glanced at the dog through the rearview mirror.

"So, did you and Brody ever finish the plan for the arch?"

"Arbor," Blay corrected her. "We are making an arbor."

"What's the difference?"

"About three days' work." Blay laughed and shook his head. "But if Mom wants an arbor for the wedding, we'll make it. I don't think it will be as hard as Brody is making it seem. Build a frame, cut the lattice to size, construct a bottom crossbar to brace, put in beading to hold the lattice, build the top of the frame, which is where the hard part comes in. Wood doesn't bend easily, but we found a weather-resistant composite material, and we can shape it into an arch. After we get that done, we slap on the facia and attach the crossbeams. Boom, arbor done. Easy. Brody's just being a pain in the ass because he has another idea for how it should be done. Mom's way is ultimately the better way."

"Why's that?"

"Because, happy mother, happy life. You don't want to piss off my mom."

Dawn rolled her eyes. "Your mom isn't that bad."

Blay turned and gawked at her. "You've obviously never seen Hover Mother activate."

"I'm sure it isn't as bad as you think."

Blay turned down the street where his childhood home was and laughed. "Brody beat us here, which means Gage has already told his grandma everything. Let me know when we go home tonight if I was wrong."

"You're worried about nothing," Dawn scoffed at him. After all, how bad could it be?

Blay parked and let his dogs out before he made his way to Dawn's side of the truck and helped her out. He dropped a soft kiss on her lips and then did it again. "If it gets too bad, come find me."

She rolled her eyes at him. "Right. Because I can't answer questions."

Blay chuckled and held her hand as they walked to the backyard gate. "She's relentless."

"She's a wonderful woman," Dawn quipped back.

"True, but I'm telling you, you don't know—"

"Blayze Benedict King."

Blay shivered and immediately turned to go back

out the gate, but Dawn caught his hand. "Ah, no, you don't, mister."

Blay groaned and turned around. "Yes, ma'am?"

Hannah King put her hands on her hips. "You've been dating for four months, and neither of you said anything?"

"I didn't because he didn't." Dawn threw him under the bus immediately, pointing at Blay as she spoke. She blinked and then looked at her newly minted exclusive boyfriend. "Blayze? You're a fireman, and your full name is Blayze? How did I not know this? Wait, Blayze Benedict King. Oh, my gawd, you're BB King?" Dawn roared with laughter. She wrapped her hands around her middle and laughed like she'd lost her faculties, but sweet heaven, it tickled her funny bone, and she needed the release.

"It isn't funny, and nobody but the Battalion Commander knows my first name at work. I'd appreciate it if they never do." Blay scrubbed his face before he leveled a pissed-off glare in his mother's direction.

"It is so funny! A firefighter named Blayze." Dawn tried to rein in her laughter and snorted, which set her off again. Her face hurt from smiling, and she tried desperately to hold her laughter.

Hannah King shrugged. "Serves you right for keeping secrets. Dawn, honey, come with me." Dawn nodded and looked at him, tried to speak, and broke into laughter again. But good Lord, it *wasn't* that funny.

She followed Hannah into the kitchen where Brody, Amber, and Gage sat around the kitchen table. "Brody, go to work."

The man had just lifted a donut to take a bite. "But…"

Hannah handed him a napkin. "Take it outside with you. Gage, honey, would you please go make sure the dogs have water in their bowls?"

"Yes, ma'am. Can I take my donut, too?"

"You already ate your donut." Amber shook her head.

"You can have another, sweetheart." Hannah smiled at Amber, who rolled her eyes.

Gage looked at his mom. "Grandma's house, Grandma's rules." The boy grabbed a frosted donut and made a beeline to the door.

"I believe those dogs are going to tackle him and eat it." Hannah grabbed the coffee pot and a cup, setting them down on the table. "All right, my dear, come sit down."

Dawn did and sipped the hot coffee Hannah

poured her. "Heaven." She loved coffee but rarely made it for just herself. What she needed was one of those pod thingies that made a single cup at a time.

"Dawn?" Hannah's question jerked her wandering mind back to the present.

"Sorry, I was thinking about the coffee and got sidetracked."

"So, I'd love to hear how you and Blay started dating." Hannah pushed the platter with a variety of donuts on it in her direction. She took one and accepted a napkin from her sister. "Well, when I first started coming over here with Amber and Gage, we started talking. He's a nice person, but then I went to the Celtic Cock with Amber and Kallie one night, and I saw him in his natural habitat, you know? The firefighter chippies were all over him, and he wasn't complaining. So, I asked around, and Blay was a known player. I'm over that. When Amber and Gage were living with me, I never had a serious relationship. It wasn't in the cards; we were a team, and we were doing okay. When things changed for her and I had time to myself, I realized that I didn't want the random one-off dates anymore. So, when Blay asked me out, I said no."

Hannah sighed. "You know, I hate hearing what I

suspected was true. Blay is a good-looking man, but I thought I raised him better."

Dawn snorted. "Hannah, he's done nothing that your other sons haven't done."

The woman blinked and sat back in her chair, cocking her head. "I guess you're right."

"I am." Dawn took another sip of her coffee.

"If you said no, how did you start dating?" Amber asked and grabbed a donut.

"According to Blay, he asked four hundred-fifty-seven times."

Amber laughed and caught a crumble of the donut's frosting as it dropped. "That is an oddly specific number."

"True. So, we went out to dinner and a movie. We already knew each other, knew we liked each other. He asked if I'd go out with him again the next time he was off shift, and I said yes. We started texting and calling. When he was on shift and Amber and Brody couldn't watch the beasts because of work, I'd go over and take them out and then run with them. We got closer, and we're now exclusive." She stared at her sister with those last words. Amber's smile was hidden by the piece of donut she popped into her mouth.

"But why didn't you tell anyone?" Hannah leaned forward and poured more coffee into her cup.

"I think Blay wanted to keep me from this. He called it the Hover Mother Inquisition."

Hannah's back went ramrod straight. "I would never!"

Amber reached out, placing a hand on the woman's arm before she added, " I think he was more concerned about his brothers' reaction. But Brody took it well. Minus one threat I'm told he lobbed."

Hannah relaxed a bit. "If Brody knows, Brock does too."

Amber snorted. "Brody didn't even wait to get home. He called Brock as soon as we got in the car to go home last night. Those men gossip more than... well, more than we do."

"Well, I'm delighted that you're dating my son. I couldn't think of a better woman for him."

Dawn smiled at Hannah. "He's used to strong women in his life. His mom raised him right. I think he likes the fact that I'm independent."

Hannah smiled. "Thank you. The good Lord knows I tried. Now, ladies, should we head to the garage and get the supplies? The others will be here in about a half-hour."

Dawn downed the rest of her coffee and stood up. "Put us to work, Hannah."

"Indeed, I will. Give me a second to put on my tennis shoes."

Amber waited until Hannah walked down the hall before she hissed, "Are you crazy? Hover Mother? That was a no-filter moment, Dawn."

She narrowed her eyes at her sister. "I don't have filters, and I'm not going to lie. That is what Blay said. I like Hannah. She has a golden heart and only wants to help, but I don't doubt she could be all up in my business if I let her. So, I'm not going to let her."

"Good luck with that," Amber chuckled. "But you're right. She's a wonderful woman."

Hannah came back down the hall, now wearing tennis shoes. "All right, ladies, we need to form an assembly line to get the planters and vases painted, and then we are popping the wine and working on centerpieces."

"Are the silk flowers here?"

"Brie and Bekki are picking them up. Sharon and her girls will be over shortly, too."

Dawn shook her head. "You don't do anything by half measures, do you, Hannah?"

The woman threw a hand up in the air and marched toward the door while she answered, "Half measures are good for baking, not life. Grab the bull by the horns, girls. Follow me."

Blay watched his mother and girlfriend walk into the house. He scrubbed his face and groaned.

"Well, son, looks like you're in the doghouse," Chauncey King said from the garden shed behind him.

He turned and walked over to where his father was pulling lawn furniture out for everyone to use today. "I didn't know my dating was that big of a deal." Which was a big fat lie.

His dad laughed, "Trying to convince yourself?"

"Yeah, probably," he admitted. His mom was always asking if he'd found a girlfriend with whom he could settle down, but she hadn't been crazy into the other's lives once they found someone, so maybe now she'd let off on the pressure. He grabbed an Adirondack chair and moved it to its place.

"She loves you, son, and wants you to be happy." Chauncey placed a chair by him, and they walked back to the shed together.

"I know. I don't want her to upset Dawn."

"Ah, well, I don't think that will happen. Dawn is a person to speak her mind."

Blay shook his head. After the baby bomb he dropped on her last night and the condom that broke, he figured he was on thin ice. Not that she said that, but damn it, troubles always came in threes.

"Blay?"

His father's voice roused him. "Sorry, what did you say?"

His father put down the chair he was holding. "You know you can tell me anything that's bothering you, right?"

Blay blinked and nodded. "Sure. Why?"

His father picked up the chair and started walking. Blay followed suit and grabbed a chair, trailing his dad. "Because for the last couple of months or so, you've been different. Almost as if the weight of the world was on your shoulders."

"Have I?" He sat his chair down and managed to look at his father, hopefully without the guilt and desperation he felt. Ellen's crazy was getting worse. His phone had been blowing up in his pocket all morning.

His father crossed his arms and stared at him. "The only thing that is going to save you from this conversation is the fact Brody and Gage have just come out of the house. We will talk today. Understand?"

He dipped his head and swallowed hard. His father was his hero. He couldn't tell him what was going on with Ellen, and he couldn't lie to him either. So, for the rest of the day, he'd avoid being alone with his dad. A mission which, by the looks of the people flooding over from the McBride's house, wouldn't be difficult.

Blay headed back to the storage shed and grabbed another chair. Brody grabbed one as Gage ran by and started talking to his grandpa.

"Ma icked me out of da itchen."

Blay did a double-take. Whatever Brody had just said was a mumbled mishmash of syllables and sounds, not words. *Ah, that's it.* His brother's mouth was stuffed full. "What are you eating?"

Brody chewed some more and finally swallowed. "A donut."

"Why did you shove all of it in your mouth? Hell of an example for your kid."

"Screw you, Poindexter. I shoved half of it in my mouth to pick up a chair and help your ass."

"Don't hold your breath waiting for a thank you. Did you bring the lumber and materials?" Blay couldn't wait to start work on the arbor. It would keep him busy all day and out of his dad's sights.

"Yeah, Dad and I unloaded it. Over there." Brody tipped his chin as he bent to pick up another chair.

Blay glanced over, finally noticing the cut lumber, toolbox, power tools, and tool belts. Brody'd collected just about every tool imaginable when they worked on the apartment building he had bought as a rundown warehouse.

"Well, let's get to it. If we start now, we'll finish by dark." Blay dropped the last chair into place.

"What's the hurry?"

Blay turned to look at his brother. "Do you want to give up another off day to work on the arbor?"

Brody clapped his hands together, "Right, let's get to it."

Blay chuckled and followed along. He'd become an expert at deflecting, and didn't that say something about the last four months of his life? He rubbed the back of his neck as he walked. Yeah, it said more than he cared to admit. Maybe it was time to come clean with his family about what was happening.

CHAPTER 5

D awn took a sip of water from the chilled
bottle she was holding. She and Amber were
sharing a blanket under the massive tree in the backyard, right where the arbor would eventually be
placed. As she watched Brody and Blay work on the
structure, she took her time to ogle her boyfriend.
His broad shoulders shifted and moved as he hefted
the heavy lumber into place. The bulk of his biceps
and the V shape of his back were a beauty to behold.
Blay bent over, and Dawn's head tilted.

Oh yeah, that ass is fine, too.

"Tell me you are not macking on Blay right now."
There was laughter in Amber's voice.

"All right, I'm not macking on Blay right now."

"Liar."

Dawn shrugged and kept her eyes on her boyfriend. "Tell me you're not checking out your husband."

"Can't. I'm totally thinking dirty thoughts."

Dawn laughed and took another drink of water. "When do we start the flower stuff?"

"I'm not sure. Tara said there was a mix-up with Brie's order, so they are trying to sort it out. The pots and vases look good."

Dawn glanced over at the work they'd done. The end result was beautiful. "Are there centerpiece vases?"

"Hannah said she was using some from the church. That's where she, Sharon, and Gage are now, picking up the boxes."

"Did someone go with them? The vases could be heavy." Dawn glanced around the crowd milling around in the backyard. Some were weeding the flower beds, some were clipping hedges, and others were putting down sod in areas that had been worn bare between the houses.

"I think Chauncey and Colm went with them." Amber glanced around. "Yeah, neither one of them is here."

Kallie walked over and removed her gloves. She

flopped down into the grass and closed her eyes. "Wake me when there's more to do."

"Late night?"

Kallie opened an eye, scowling at them. "Who slept?" She closed her eyes again.

Dawn turned her attention from Blay to Kallie. "Working?"

The woman yawned and then nodded. "Yeah. A double homicide. Grant and I have worked the last seventy-two hours almost straight through, but we caught her."

"Her?" Both she and Amber spoke at the same time.

Kallie snorted but didn't open her eyes. "Thirteen-year-old daughter killed Mom and Dad because they wouldn't buy her a new cell phone. Then she ditched and couch hopped. As soon as we were able to put the word out, parents started to call. We picked up the princess at the mall, shopping with her mom's credit card."

The skin on her arms prickled, and she shuddered. "What type of person does it take to do something like that and then show no remorse? Good Lord... How can you work in a job where you face such depravity?"

Kallie rolled over onto her side and propped her

head up on her hand. "I don't do it for the murderers. I do it for the victims, both living and dead. Justice will happen in the courts, whatever that looks like, but the people who have to go on living, that have nothing but questions, those are the people I work for."

"Man, I never had a good relationship with my mother, but let me tell you, that's extreme. Is she clinical?"

Kallie snorted. "I'd say so. Her biggest concern was getting her new phone back. We Mirandized her and had a public defender there to ask her questions. She told the guy to stop interrupting her. She told us everything, even where to find the baseball bat she used to cave in their skulls while they slept. She said she was a juvenile and we couldn't charge her like an adult."

"Hey, what are y'all talking about?" Tara dropped down on the blanket.

"Thirteen-year-old bat-wielding killers," Dawn quipped.

"Oh, is that all?" Tara dropped down on her back. "If I bend over anymore today, I'm going to be permanently formed into a question mark."

"Are the beds done?"

"Mine is. Caitlyn and Bekki are almost done, and

Erin and Torin are kissing more than they are pulling weeds, but I'll let Hannah handle that when she gets back."

"Should we start some lunch or something?" Amber asked no one in particular.

Kallie yawned. "I say pizza. We can pitch in."

Dawn wrinkled her nose "Tacos. There's a joint just down the road."

"Fried Chicken," Bekki said as she and Caitlyn ambled over. "Mom, Sharon, and the dads are picking up an order on their way back from the church. At least we're not being recruited to make lunch."

"Your mom hasn't been that bad. With all of us here, the yard looks great, and we have everything else done. All we need to do this afternoon is work out the flowers." Dawn leaned back and braced herself on her hands.

"Brie should be here soon. Hopefully, she got the flower situation taken care of. Oh, and congratulations, by the way." Tara looked over at her when she spoke.

"On what?" Kallie managed to open an eye for a moment.

Bekki's eyes popped wide. "What did we miss?"

"Yeah, congrats on what?" Caitlyn asked, turning her way.

Amber turned to her and just lifted her eyebrows.

Dawn rolled her eyes. "Blay and I have been dating for about four months now."

"Oh, I thought it was something new." Kallie sighed and dropped her arm over her eyes.

"Wait, what?" Bekki looked from one person to another. "Why am I always the last to know?"

"Because you talk too much," Blay said as he approached the group.

"You, my manwhore brother, have decided to enter the adult world of relationships?"

Dawn snorted, "First, not cool calling my boyfriend a manwhore, even if it was true before he met me. Totally not cool saying it in front of me."

Bekki blinked and looked at Caitlyn.

"I'm with her." She pointed back at Dawn.

"Okay, I'm sorry I called you a manwhore in front of Dawn." Bekki batted her eyelashes.

"Second, we were keeping it to ourselves until we decided that we were going to be exclusive." Which wasn't the case, but it might make Blay's life a little easier.

"I'm stealing my girlfriend for a moment." Blay

extended his hand to her, and she took it, letting him help her get up.

They moved toward the back porch. "What's up?"

Blay pulled her into his arms and kissed her. "Nothing. I'm taking a break while Brody cusses to himself for a bit, so I thought I'd see how bad the Mom Interrogation was this morning."

Dawn wrapped her arms around his neck and laughed. "She is a wonderful person, and she's happy we're dating. Now, what she says to *you* is between the two of you." She pulled away from him when his cell phone in his pocket vibrated. "Do you need to get that?"

He pulled out his phone and flipped it to face her. Ellen's name was on the face. When it cleared, she did a double-take at the number of missed calls. *Fifty-seven calls?* "Blay, what if there is something wrong?"

He shook his head. "I listened to the first five voice messages. She's leaving the same kind of messages. Listen to the last one. I don't care. I have nothing to hide."

Dawn took the phone and tapped on the voice-mail that dropped a couple of seconds earlier. *"Blay, I'm going to move to Hope City. I can stay with you. You have enough room. I've let my landlord know that*

I'll be giving up my apartment. This way, we can be a family."

Dawn looked up at Blay. A dark slither of jealousy ran down her spine. She hit replay and let him listen to the message.

He closed his eyes and dropped his head. "What the hell?"

"I think you need to let your dad know what's happening. Maybe he knows..." *Hell, what would he know? Is it possible to get a restraining order against a possible baby momma?*

Blay sighed and dropped the phone back into his pocket. "I'll talk to him this afternoon, but I don't think there's much he can do."

"She can't just move into your apartment. Can she?" Dawn shook her head. "No, of course, she can't."

"I don't know what's going to happen to her, but she's not moving in with me. The main doors are locked, she doesn't have a key to my apartment, and the dogs would be there. If someone tries to break in, Thor will go insane."

"Yeah, okay." Dawn drew a deep breath. This thing with crazy baby momma had moved from weird to obsessive in about twenty-four hours.

"Hey, look, I'll try to keep this out of our relationship. I wasn't going to tell you about these calls. They shouldn't affect you." Blay ran a hand up her arm and cupped her cheek. "Don't let this freak you out. I'll keep it away from you."

"I'm not going to lie to you. I'm concerned, but not about me. About you. This woman is mentally unstable. It would help if you got a lawyer, a restraining order, and let your family know what's going on. You don't want them blindsided if she does something."

Blay gave a half-hearted chuckle. "She's four months pregnant. What's she going to do?"

Dawn tilted her chin up and looked at him. "Show up at your apartment with a moving truck full of stuff?"

He lifted the phone. "I'll take care of that right now. I'm going to go out front and call her to let her know not to come." He turned to walk down the path that led to the side gate.

"Wait, Blay. Don't do that."

"What?"

"I'm worried, Blay. She's lost touch with reality." Dawn crossed her arms. "Wait until your dad gets back and tell him what's happening. If he thinks you should call her, then do it and let him listen to the call. I'll be with your mom, so she won't know what's going on. It can be between the two of you until you're ready to let her know what's going on." She glanced at the tree where everyone had gathered in the shade. "They'll all find out eventually."

"Rory knows the basics, but I trust him to keep my secret." He'd grown up with the man and knew he'd keep his confidence.

"Good. Now let's grab one of those coolers and go back to the group before they figure out something is wrong." She lifted on her toes and kissed him, which was met with a loud cheer from those finding respite on the shaded lawn.

Blay bent her over backward, continuing to kiss her. Brock shouted, "Get a room," and someone else wolf-whistled. She gripped his arms to steady herself, and he slowly returned her to upright, still kissing her. When he lifted away, she sighed and dropped her head to his chest.

"I'll handle it. I promise." Blay kissed the top of her head, and they grabbed the ice chest with the drinks. There was another round of cheers, this time for the cool beverages.

When they found a piece of shade, she leaned back on his chest, fitted between his legs. The feeling was so easy, and it felt *right*. She was getting in deep with this man. Warning bells that usually fired were strangely silent. The desire to cut ties laid dormant. Even with the drama surrounding the woman from his past, the seemingly ever-present need to rehearse the 'it isn't you, it's me' speech hadn't bubbled to the surface. She took a drink of Blay's beer and passed it back to him.

"We leave for an hour, and you take a nap." Hannah's laughed reprimand came from the porch.

Brock lifted his head from where he and Kallie were dozing. "Unless you have food, we're on strike."

"Well, then I'm in luck. Fried chicken, potato and macaroni salad, peach cobbler, and a restock on the beer." Hannah announced the menu as her husband and Colm McBride trundled out with huge boxes.

Gage raced toward them and flopped on Brock. His uncle gave a grunt and then moaned and acted as if he was trying to get up when Gage pinned him. Brody got to his knees and slapped the lawn, shouting, "One, two, three!" Gage got up and danced around with his hands up in the air.

Tara's daughter, Colleen, hopped out of the house and shouted at the top of her lungs, "Grandma said to wash your hands, or you don't get lunch!"

Tara sighed heavily. "You can tell the conversations we've had about inside voices worked, right?"

Her husband, Carter, chuckled and stood,

offering his wife a hand. "Technically, she was outside."

Sean McBride echoed Carter's sentiment. "I remember someone else who liked to yell. She grew up to have a daughter that was just like her."

Tara shot Sean a look. "Don't forget, I know your secrets. I'll tell your wife."

Sean put his hand out to help up Harper, his wife. He smiled at her as she stood. "She's lying, dear. I'm an angel."

Harper chortled and brushed some grass off her shorts. "Don't forget, I know your mother, and she's already told me all your secrets."

Dawn and Blay laughed as they stood. She adored this conjoined family. Since they were last, she bumped into Blay, drawing his attention. She whispered, "Don't forget to talk to your dad."

He winked at her and mouthed, *I promise.* She'd accept the answer and put that worry to rest. The ball was in Blay's court, not hers. Somehow, she knew that mantra would come in handy.

Blay approached his father and Colm, who were visiting in the shade of the back porch. "Hey, Dad, do you have a couple of minutes?"

"Of course. Colm, excuse us?" His father dipped into the cooler and handed Blay a soda. All serious conversations with his dad had always come with a soda chaser. It was his father's thing.

"Maybe out front?" His dad nodded toward the walkway. Blay followed his father, wishing for the fifty or sixtieth time today he didn't have to break this news to him, but Dawn was right. Ellen had gone too far.

They rounded the corner and sat down on rockers that had always occupied the front porch during the summer months. "What's going on?"

Blay snapped the top of his soda open and took a sip. "About four months ago, a woman I had, ah, spent time with called me out of the blue and told me that she was pregnant and the baby was mine."

His father leaned forward and placed his elbows on his knees. He turned his head and looked at Blay. "Is it?"

"See, that's just it. I asked for a paternity test because if the kid is mine, I'm going to step up, you know? But she went hysterical and threw me out of her apartment. I hired a detective because I'm careful, Dad. Very careful. I don't think the baby is mine. The detective followed her to the doctor and confirmed she is pregnant. Since then, she's gone off the deep end."

He pulled out his phone and opened the text app. They sat in silence as his father scrolled and read. Finally, his father handed it back.

"That's not all." He opened the voicemail and played him the one that Dawn and he'd listened to earlier.

His dad scrolled through the voicemails, looking at the amount and the dates. "Well, I'm going to recommend you get a restraining order. It won't stop her from making contact, but it will give you ammunition to use in court if it comes to that. Has she made trouble for you? The text messages were troubling, to say the least."

"No sir, not yet. Dawn is uncomfortable, but she's willing to stick around. That was my primary concern. Ellen's threatened a lot, but so far, the only one she's contacted is me."

"Who's being threatened?" Brock asked as he rounded the corner. Brody was right beside him. Blay sighed and looked at his father. His dad shrugged, allowing him to sweep it under the carpet, but he knew his brothers wouldn't have it.

Blay took a drink of his soda and repeated the story, surrendering his phone for his brothers to examine. Brock handed the phone to Brody and sat down on the steps. "Kallie and I have first-hand experience with stalkers, as you well know."

"Ellen isn't stalking me. She's just an annoyance."

Brock shook his head as Brody sat down. "I talked to several of the department's psychiatrists. This is a typical profile of a stalker. This unwanted contact and attention coupled with the harassment of the texts and messages is a stalker, Blay. First, you need to make a police report and then you need to file for a restraining order. I'm not joking. She could have a mental illness, personality disorder, or a substance abuse problem."

Blay snapped back in his chair. "She's pregnant. Do you think she'd be using?"

Brody nodded. "I see it all the time. Junkies only crave the next high and have a reckless disregard for the kid."

Blay scrubbed his face. "Okay, I'll file a report on this, but I don't want the ladies to know about it."

Brock looked from his father to him. "Does Dawn know?"

"Yeah, of course. I wanted to be one hundred percent up-front with her. If this baby is mine, which I doubt, I want to make sure that it has a good life, and if that means going to court to take it away from her, I will."

"The courts don't take parental rights away easily, especially from the mother." His father leaned back and rocked in the chair while he spoke.

"I know. I've been saving all of these texts and voicemails on the cloud." Blay sighed and shook his head. "I've been with her twice. Both times we met up at the Celtic Cock. She's a firefighter chippie. The last time I almost had to carry her out of the apartment. It was bad."

"So, she knows where you live?" Brock asked.

"Yeah, which has Dawn worried about this voicemail." He pushed play and let his brothers listen. "We can alert the other tenants and remind them not to let anyone in that they don't personally know," Blay suggested.

"The dogs will stop her from going in," Brock added.

"She didn't meet the dogs when she was there?"

"No, I brought her home the long weekend you, Amber, and Gage took them up to Cunningham Falls State Park."

"Well, that works in your favor. I agree with Brock. You need to document this with a police report. It will save you headaches down the road. We all know a restraining order is as good as the paper it's written on, but again, if she violates it, it can be documented and used later on." His father pushed the rocking chair gently. "I'm not thrilled about keeping secrets from your mom, but knowing her, she'd worry herself sick, so I'm going to make an exception this time. But we will tell her and the girls if this woman does anything other than leave you text and voice messages. As Brock said, there are different types of stalkers. We're hoping she's harmless, but we have to accept there is a possibility she has mental health issues."

"Thanks." Blay looked at each of his brothers and father in return.

His dad stood up. "That's what family is for, son. Brock, will you run him down to the precinct and get the process started?"

"What? Now?"

"You're working a twenty-four tomorrow, right?" His father looked at him and waited for a response.

"Yes, sir."

"Then now. Brock, make sure the paperwork for a restraining order gets done, too. I'll make a call to Judge Abrams. He'll approve it when he sees the phone logs."

"You got it. Come on, let's go."

"Wait, we haven't finished the arbor." Brody's eyes narrowed. "You promised we'd get this done in a day."

"Don't worry, Killian is coming this afternoon. We'll have it up before you know it." His dad clamped Brody on the shoulder and turned him around. Brock chuckled and pulled out his phone. "I'm texting Kallie to let her know I'll be back in a couple of hours. It would be best if you did the same. I've learned keeping the significant other informed makes for a smooth home life."

Blay pulled out his phone and explained what he was doing to Dawn. Her immediate reply:

> *Good. Take your time. Flowers and wine here. No rush.*

Blay got into Brock's old truck and slammed the door shut. He hated filing a police report, but the cops in his family weren't knee-jerk types of people. His phone vibrated once again, and he dropped his head back on the headrest. If serving her with a restraining order would get her to stop contacting him, the trip this afternoon would be worth it.

CHAPTER 6

Dawn glanced down at her vibrating phone as she typed. She didn't recognize the number, but that was nothing new. Working as the headquarters office manager for HRNC Trucking and Warehousing, her number was public information. She grabbed it, swiped the face, and tucked it between her ear and her shoulder as she continued to type. "This is Dawn."

There was no one on the other end. She grabbed the phone and looked at the screen. The call was connected. She tried again, "Hello, this is Dawn. Can I help you?" Nothing. She hung up and went back to work.

"Hey, Dawn. Let's call it quits for the day." Her boss, Clyde, walked out of his office and flicked off his lights. She glanced up at the clock. It was already seven-thirty. Blay was working his twenty-four-hour shift, so she didn't have any reason to rush home, but still, she hadn't even noticed how late it was. "Wow, where has today gone?"

"I don't know. I looked up, and we were the only two in the office. Come on, save what you're working on, and I'll walk you out."

She rolled her shoulders and glanced at the data she was inputting into the spreadsheet. "Okay, just let me mark this." She marked her stopping point by highlighting the column and closed the four spreadsheets and two documents she was pulling information from. The report wasn't due to the bank until Friday, so she had time. She shut down her computer and stood, stretching her back. "Did Amber call you today?"

"Yes, I have an appointment with them on Wednesday. She explained a little of what they believe is going on. If there is criminal activity happening, I need to know. We can close that warehouse location down and refurbish and rebrand it into the HRNC family earlier than anticipated if they have to make arrests. Perhaps the best-case scenario. Those people you let go last week have flooded my inbox with complaint emails."

"God, mine, too, and I've been getting weird phone calls since I let them go. Well, since just after. Hang-ups and a crackpot just being silent or breathing on the line." She shook her head. "I don't understand how they feel we need to give them another chance. Stealing is stealing. They were provided training and their copy of the employee handbook like everyone else."

"The sense of entitlement is strong with this last company, but we've gone through worse. Oh, Paul wanted to know if you'd like to come over this weekend and spend some time by the pool with us. Fair warning, he has a friend he's going to try to set you up with."

Dawn laughed and waited by the front doors as her boss locked up behind them. They didn't set the alarm because there were two cars other than theirs in the parking lot. Probably the IT folks who always had some update to push. The front doors were locked from six at night to six in the morning, though. "Well, in fair warning, I have a boyfriend."

Clyde snapped upright, forgetting his key in the lock. "Really?"

She laughed at the comical look of hope that covered his face. "Yes, really. He's a firefighter."

Clyde grabbed his key, locked the door, and

pocketed his ring of keys. They turned toward the parking lot. "Where are you parked?"

"Way out in the south forty. I forgot training was pulling everyone in for certifications this morning." She nodded to the back corner of the parking lot, where the lights barely reached.

"I'll walk you, and you can tell me all about your young man."

"You don't have to walk me. I'm a big girl now." She smiled at him.

"And you're not getting out of it without sharing details that I can give to Paul. He's going to want to be sure you're not inventing a fake guy to get out of the weekend." He winked at her. His husband was notorious for trying—and failing—to fix up his friends.

"Well, his name is Blay, and he's six foot six inches tall. He has dark brown hair, almost black, with ice blue eyes. He's part of a huge family. Three boys and two girls. His mother is a riot, and his dad is a silver fox, so I think he's going to age well." She laughed and shook her head. "Seriously though, he's kind, attentive, and fun. I really like him."

He turned and walked backward, talking to her, "You've met the 'rents already?"

"I've known them for a while now. Two weeks

ago, we were all over at the house getting ready for that wedding I asked for time off for, remember? I want to be available to help on Friday with the last-minute details of the wedding, which is on Saturday."

"Yeah, yeah, I remember. So, back on topic, is he hot?" Clyde asked.

"You know, as my employer, you shouldn't be asking me that." She laughed when he grunted.

"I'm asking for Paul. Legally, he can ask." His comment was a bit too innocent to be true.

"No, he isn't hot. He's *nuclear*. The chiseled body of a god and the stamina of a firefighter." She fanned herself with her hand, laughing until she looked at her car. "Oh, shit."

Clyde looked at her. "What?"

She pointed to her car. All four tires were flat. *Oh, no.* Her front window was bashed in as they moved closer. She saw the word BITCH scratched into her hood. The tail lights were also smashed. "Who… what… damn it." She dropped her head. "Just what I need."

"Son of a bitch. This isn't on you. I'll pay for everything and get a tow truck out here to get it to the garage we use for the company trucks." Clyde was already scrolling through his phone.

"No, that's okay. I have insurance." The little crossover hybrid wasn't a Rolls, but she liked it.

"Which you shouldn't have to use. This is the work of my disgruntled ex-employees. My insurance should cover this mess. Tomorrow, I'll have the grounds crew start the paperwork for a new lighting system out here. We should have taken care of this before now." Clyde was talking to himself more than her.

She put a hand on his forearm. "You can't take the blame for this happening."

He lifted his attention away from the phone and looked at her. "I know, but I can prevent it from happening again. Let's head back to the office. I'm going to let you use my company truck until this is taken care of."

"You don't need to do that. I have a rental car rider on my insurance."

"Which you are not going to use. Just replace any gas you use and log the miles in the logbook."

"Are you sure?" She didn't want to put her boss out.

"Positive. Besides, the new wrap on that truck is amazing. You'll be my new advertising system."

She laughed and turned to walk back with him. Of all the places she could work, HRNC was the best, even if spiteful ex-employees reared their ugly heads.

An hour later, she pulled the truck into her driveway and put it into park. She'd driven Blay's truck once or twice when he'd blocked her in the driveway and she needed to pop out to the store, and thank goodness she had. This four-wheel-drive truck had a wide turn radius like Blay's. She dropped out of the vehicle and hit the key fob, locking it. She let herself into her little house and headed to the kitchen. A glass of wine first, then she'd rummage through the refrigerator and make herself a late dinner.

She stepped out of her wedge heels and wiggled her toes on the cold tile. She'd finally decided to take the morning-after pill after a long discussion with Blay. It was her decision, but she wanted his input.

Her phone rang in her purse. She stopped halfway to the fridge and backtracked to her purse, which she'd left on the table by the front door. After she fished it out, she answered it in her usual way, "Hello, handsome." Then she turned on her heel and padded back to the refrigerator and her self-promised glass of wine.

"Hey, you. How was your day?" His deep, sexy voice was music to her ears.

She pulled an open bottle of Chardonnay out of the door. "Dear Lord, it was insane. Yours?"

"Believe it or not, we haven't had a call out in almost eight hours. I got some decent studying in and worked out. I also found out none of the people we pulled out of that apartment building made it."

"Oh, Blay, Amber told me that on Sunday. Brody had talked to Sean. I was going to tell you, but I forgot." She closed her eyes. "I'm so sorry."

"No worries. It was better to hear it here. Sean, Brody, or Amber could have told me on Sunday, but they probably thought I already knew. I was able to process it and work through the response with the other teams along with the Battalion Commander."

"Good. What about PBM?" They'd shortened psycho baby momma to an acronym somehow, but it worked.

"No text, no voicemail. Thank God. What was so insane about today?"

"Well, I'm doing that financial report for the company's bank."

"You said something about that last night. So, why do they need a report? Can't they just check his accounts?"

She laughed, "If only. Clyde is planning to purchase another trucking line, and they want a complete consolidated listing of our assets and liabilities. So, I'm compiling the documents the sub-companies are sending in. Then, when I walked out to my car, we found out one of the employees we let go last week decided to take out their frustration on my car. Four flat tires, a not nice word scratched into my hood, and the windshield and brake lights bashed in."

"Ah, hell. I'm sorry that happened, babe. Are you okay?"

She poured her wine into the goblet-sized glass she'd pulled down from the cupboard. "I'm fine. Pissed, but what can you do? Idiots want to retaliate for me firing them. It happens; granted, it is usually just a vicious email or something like that. So, these guys are overachievers. They've sent me and Clyde emails. I'm getting the ghosted telephone calls and then tonight my car. He called the police as soon as we got back to the office. "

"So, you filed a police report? Good. Your insurance company is going to need one," Blay replied, assuming she was going to file a report.

"Clyde wants me to let him file with his insurance agency since it happened on his property."

"That's nice of him."

"Money isn't an issue for him. He and his husband don't have a lot of close friends, so those they have, they smother." She took a sip of her wine and slipped down into a chair at the kitchen table. "I'd love to introduce you to them. They are good people."

"I'd like to meet—" The station's klaxon siren sounded, and she jerked the phone away from her ear. "Got to go. Love you."

The connection ended, and she stared at the phone.

Love you?

Dawn lifted the glass of wine to her lips and downed it. *Love you.* Just over four months into a relationship. *Who drops the L word like that?* She poured herself another glass of wine and stared at the phone now sitting on the table. Wasn't there supposed to be a significant build-up to saying those words? Some huge romantic gesture? She got up, went back to the refrigerator, and pulled out leftovers.

A bold, romantic gesture so wasn't her scene, though. She wasn't a chocolate and flowers kind of gal. She'd rather Blay help her build a stepping stone path at the side of the house than being wined and dined. But the L word was a big step. Miles bigger than them both agreeing to be exclusive, and that was just a few weeks ago.

She put her cold chicken and rice into the microwave and punched in two minutes, starting the process of warming her food. She lifted the wine to her lips and paused before she took a sip. The question she'd failed to ask herself was did *she* love *Blay*? She gazed out the kitchen window, staring at a streetlight across the street. Was what she felt for him love? When he wasn't here, the desire to be with him could be marked down to lust, true, but it wasn't just about the sex. Granted, that was awesome, but she loved spending time with him. Even if the time they spent was them vegged out in front of the television, she coveted it. When they weren't together, it was as if a part of her was missing. She thought of him when something struck her as funny. She wanted to share her day with him and wanted to know how he was, how his work had gone, and to be there for him when things were tough. Was that love?

She pulled out her food when the beeper sounded and sat down at the table to eat. Her mom and dad were the best examples of love she'd ever witnessed. Her dad was also Amber's dad. He'd divorced Amber's mom and married Dawn's mother. In the time they were married, she'd witnessed the gentleness of love and the bond between them. She moved her chicken around her plate as she thought. Did she have that level of unity and emotional bond with Blay?

Dawn leaned back in her seat and sipped her wine. No, not yet, but it was a close thing. He was the spark that ignited her engine. All the pieces of her life fell together and worked like magic with that spark. Without it, she'd gone through the motions of the day. She'd had a purpose when Amber and Gage lived here but she didn't have her own life. She'd put that on hold to help her sister raise a great kid.

When they first moved out, she'd gone a bit crazy and went out on dates she'd swiped right on. Some were a disaster, some weren't, but none were... well, none were Blay. Blayze. She chuckled and picked up her fork. If he repeated it, would she? A small smile split her lips. Yeah, she would. She'd fallen for the man like a lead balloon falls from the sky. Hard, fast, and without a chance of stopping.

CHAPTER 7

Hannah King spun from the kitchen sink when the doorbell rang. It wasn't Sharon because she'd walk through the back door. She grabbed a tea towel and dried her hands as she walked to the front door. She checked through the peephole. A young woman, blonde hair and blue eyes, stood at the door. Hannah opened the door. "May I help you?"

The woman smiled at her and patted her belly—correction, her baby bump. "Hi, Mrs. King? Blay's mom?"

Hanna looked from the woman's face to her belly and back again. An eyebrow lifted on its own accord as she pieced together what was happening. "Yes?"

"I'm Ellen, his fiancée."

And that was the woman's first strike. One thing Hannah King couldn't abide by was a liar. "Really?"

"Well, we haven't announced it yet. May I come in?" The woman walked past her, breaking the door from her grip.

Hannah followed the woman into her formal living room. Family pictures were scattered in silver frames that she'd inherited from her mother. "Oh, is this your grandson?"

Hannah crossed her arms. "What do you want?"

"To meet my baby's family." The woman rubbed her small bump and continued to move around the room. She stopped in front of a small Tiffany lamp her great-grandmother had passed down to her. "Nice? Tiffany?"

Hannah stared at the woman, not answering.

"I'll be moving in with Blay soon. I wanted you to know that."

"And what about his girlfriend?" Hannah watched the woman jerk as if she'd been hit.

She went pale and sat down. "What?"

"I know his girlfriend. She's wonderful. I don't know you. Who are you, and why are you here?"

"I'm going to marry Blay. We're going to have a baby. He's in love with me."

"Then why hasn't he mentioned you or the baby to me?"

"That's a lie!" The woman shouted the words as she sprung up from the couch.

"No, it isn't. There is one thing in this life I will not do, and that is tell a lie. My son doesn't love you. If he did, he'd have brought you home and introduced you to us." She watched as the words sank in.

Her unwelcome and bizarre visitor cast her eyes around the room. "It's a shame. You seem to enjoy family."

"My family is my life." It was the truth.

A smug smile spread across the blonde's face. "Mine too. Mark my words, Mrs. King, your son will marry me. He is the baby's father, after all."

Hannah snorted. "Not until I see the paternity test he isn't."

And that wasn't the right thing to say. The blonde hit a side table lamp and sent it crashing to the ground. "Bitch, if you're not careful, you'll never see this baby *or* Blay. I'll take them both away from you."

Hannah stepped back and pointed to the door. "Leave. Take your threats and baseless insinuations and leave. You are not welcome here, and you'll never be welcome in this house."

"I tried to be nice." The woman ambled past her as she spoke.

"Just one question." Hannah's words stopped the blonde at the front door. "Do you know what my husband does for a living?"

The woman shrugged. "Does it matter? He has money. I can tell by your house." She opened the screen door and walked out.

Hannah race-walked to the front door and memorized the vehicle's license plate the woman was driving before she locked the front door and headed for her telephone. She pushed her speed dial and tapped her fingers as the phone went to voicemail. "Blayze, I just had an unexpected visitor from someone who claims to be carrying your child. Call me back. Now."

She drew several shaky breaths and grabbed a piece of paper and pen. While she waited for Blay to call her, she wrote down the license plate number and every word she could remember of the confrontation. Well, she might be an advanced-to-older middle-aged woman, but *this* woman was married to the Chief of Police, and while she might be the busybody everyone accused her of being, she wasn't a pushover. If that Ellen person messed with her family, she was going to meet a side of her she'd only shown Chauncey's mother. Nobody messed with her family.

Nobody.

Her phone rang, and she glanced at the name displayed. "Are you working?"

Blay answered, "No, ma'am, and I'm on my way over now. I can explain everything."

"Is that baby yours?"

There was a pause on the other end of the line. "I'll explain everything when I get there, Mom."

"That wasn't an answer." The fight seeped out of her.

"It isn't what you think. Just don't judge me and find me guilty until I explain everything. Call Dad and tell him what happened, please."

She closed her eyes. "Your father knows what is going on?"

"Yes, ma'am. I've filed a restraining order against Ellen. Don't let her back in the house. I think she's unbalanced. Have you locked the door?"

"I have." She glanced at the back door and got up to lock it, too.

"Call Dad. I'm driving as fast as I can."

"Be safe, Blay," she cautioned him and then said goodbye.

Dialing a number she knew by heart, she waited

for the phone to be answered. "Chief King's office. This is Helene."

"Helene, it's Hannah. I need to speak to Chauncey."

"He's in a meeting right now."

"Helene, this is a 911 call." She'd only used that code one other time, when Brody had been T-boned in that intersection.

"Just a second."

Not fifteen seconds later, Chauncey answered the phone with a brisk, "What's happened?"

"Blay told me to call you. The woman he has a restraining order against forced her way into our house about ten minutes ago. Chauncey, she's... she's pregnant, and I think she's mad. Insane. I wrote everything down, and I have her license plate number."

"Good. That's good, honey. I'm going to call Colm and have him come over until I can get there. I'm in a meeting with the mayor. I'll shake it as soon as I can."

"Okay." She stared at the paper where she'd scrawled the words the woman had spewed. "Is that baby Blay's?" God, she prayed not. He'd be tied to that woman for the rest of his life. She formed a fist with her free hand, trying to stop the shaking that had suddenly started.

"I don't know. Have you called Blay?"

"He's on his way over."

"He'll explain everything. Colm will come to sit with you until I get home. You did the right thing, Hannah. I love you."

She closed her eyes and drew the first deep breath in the last fifteen minutes. "I love you, too." She hung up and stared at the words, going through everything the woman said. She jumped at the knock at the back door. Colm and Sharon were standing on the porch. She stood up and opened the door.

"What's happening?" Colm strode through the house as his wife asked the question.

"I'm making sure the house is locked up."

Sharon turned to Hannah. "Why?"

Hannah let a tear slip down her cheek. "I wish I knew."

Blay sat across the kitchen table from his mother and father. Colm and Sharon had left as soon as Blay had gotten home. He'd explained everything to his mother, showed her the text messages, and let her listen to a sample of the voicemails, all of which stopped the moment he told Ellen he'd filed a restraining order and the cops were looking for her. "I thought I'd heard the last of this."

"A baby doesn't go away." His mother's level stare held his.

"I know, and when I know for sure that it's mine, I'll do everything I can do to give that child a normal life."

"Even if it means saddling yourself with that woman?"

Confused, he leaned forward. "I'll never marry her, Mom."

His mother leaned forward and hit the kitchen table with a single finger. "You don't have to marry her to be saddled with her. Every time you talk to your child, every child support payment, every visit, birthday, holiday, every time you have any interaction with that baby, you'll have to deal with *her*. You can't ignore her. She's the mother."

"And if I have my way about it, I'll sue her for full custody." Blay's voice lifted to match his mom's.

"Right. Okay, suppose for just a moment that the courts grant you custody. How are you going to raise an infant? You're a firefighter. Is Dawn going to take on another woman's baby again?" Hannah lifted her finger off the table and slowly crossed her arms. "Do you have the right to ask her to do that?"

Blay dropped his head into his hands. "I don't have the right, but Mom, I love Dawn, and I'm pretty sure she loves me." He'd let that little secret out of the bag three nights ago when he'd hung up. Like a chicken shit, he'd pretended it hadn't happened during his two extra shifts. He wanted to see her when he brought it up to know for sure that she was where he was in this relationship.

"Hell of a way to start a relationship," Hannah huffed. "This woman is not well, Blay. The good news is she doesn't know who your father is. She thinks we have money. She knew what the Tiffany lamp was, and she took inventory of the silver frames."

His phone rang, and he pulled it from his back pocket. "Excuse me. This is the BC." He slid his finger and answered the call. "King."

His eyes darted to his father as he listened. "No sir, that's a bald-faced lie. I have a restraining order against her. No, sir, I deny it completely. I've never lifted a hand against her. I haven't seen her in over three months. Sir, she was just here to see my mother, uninvited. Mom, did she have any bruises, a black eye?"

"Absolutely not. She's on the front door camera. We can prove it." Hannah swung her attention to her husband as Blay repeated the information.

"Sir, ask her when I supposedly did this to her." The woman answered, and the Battalion Chief repeated her answer. "Sir, you can check with Captain Hayes. I covered Bailey's shift. His wife had her baby. I pulled three shifts in a row so he could have time with his wife and kid. That's why I'm off today." Blay covered the mic. "She's backpedaling. I can hear her." He closed his eyes as her voice changed from plaintive to snarling and vicious. He held the phone from his ear, and his mother's eyes popped open wide before she pursed her lips and nodded.

"King?"

Blay put the phone back against his ear. "Yes, sir?"

"Tell me you have a running police report going on this woman."

"Yes, sir, I do. I'll be amending the restraining order to include my family and work."

"Do that. I'll document this. Charleston was in the office with me. She'll write a statement, too." His BC's policy was to always have a chaperone in the room with him when he was talking to a civilian female, no matter who she was. It paid off this time.

He disconnected the call and looked across the table at his father. "Dad, the BC had a witness. They're both writing statements." He turned to his mom. "Dawn is my worry, Mom. If this child is mine, I will do everything I can to nurture both relationships, but in the end, that baby is my responsibility, and I will take care of him or her, alone if need be."

She stared at him for a long minute. "You're a good man, Blayze. You'll never be alone. We will help."

He smiled at her and reached across for her hand. "I know, Mom, but just like I can't ask Dawn to take on my child, I can't ask you."

Hannah smiled. "You didn't ask, I volunteered, and I'd be surprised if Dawn didn't do the same thing."

His father stood up. "Now that the fences are mended, I'm going to call in and get a patrol over to your station to get those statements. I'll call in a few favors and see if I can get that restraining order amended, too."

"What about Dawn?" Hannah gripped his hand tightly. "Do you think this woman would do something stupid like approach Dawn?"

Blay scrubbed his face with his free hand. "I don't

know. I'm going to her house tonight. I'll bring her up to speed." He glanced at his father. "Can we include significant others in the order?"

His dad shrugged, "I'll see what I can do. At this point, in my opinion, she's a safety concern. I'd like the force's forensic psychologist to take a look at the statement your mom and the people at the station are making. The texts and voicemails, too, if you'll allow access to where they're stored."

"Absolutely." Blay nodded. He'd do anything to remove Ellen from his life. The baby, on the other hand... He sighed. His child would grow up knowing love and his family. No matter what it took to make that happen, he'd make it work.

Somehow.

CHAPTER 8

Dawn stopped the truck before she turned into her driveway. Blay's truck was there, and she wasn't sure if she could maneuver the beast she was driving onto the driveway with his truck there, too. A polite beep of a horn behind her forced her hand. She pulled in and held her breath as she drove. If she got too close to his truck, he couldn't get in or out, and if she moved over too far, her rose bushes would pay the price. She put the truck into park and opened the driver's side door. Every bush was intact.

Blay opened his truck's door and laughed. "You said you had a company vehicle; you didn't say it was a truck."

She jumped down from the seat and reached

back for the groceries and her purse. "It isn't a truck. It's a truck on steroids, just like yours. Me man, me want to crush other cars." She growled the last part and held her hands with the bags dangling from them as she walked up to him.

"Oh, is that what you think of my baby here?" He patted the hood of his truck.

"Yep. Boys and toys. They get bigger with age." She lifted onto her toes and kissed him. "Why are you waiting out here?"

He took the grocery bags from her. "The key isn't under the flowerpot."

She frowned and headed over to the brightly painted pot under the kitchen window. "It should be." She lifted the pot where it lived. "That is weird." On a hunch, she lifted the larger pot that sat next to it. "Ah, here you are." She stood and held the key up. "It migrated."

Blay lifted an eyebrow. "Keys are inanimate objects. They don't move by themselves."

Dawn rolled her eyes. "I know that. Amber must have moved it when she came over to get Gage's tennis shoes the other day."

"Doesn't she have a key?" Blay followed her into the house when she opened the door with the spare key.

"Yeah, but if she leaves the car running, she uses this one." She tossed the key onto the counter and stepped out of her heels. "Oh, man, that feels so good. How was your day off? Did you get all your errands done?" He'd pulled a triple shift so one of the guys he worked with could be home with his wife and new baby until her mom could get to town.

Blay put the groceries on the counter and shook his head. "Not everything. There was an incident today at my mom and dad's."

She froze with a package of chicken in her hand. "What? Is everyone okay?"

He nodded, and she released the air caught in her lungs. "Next time, lead with that little bit of information, okay? What type of incident?" She turned and headed to the fridge with the chicken and a pint of cream.

"Ellen showed up there."

She paused at the door as the implications hit her. "Wait, your mom doesn't know."

"She does now." Blay took the chicken and cream from her and put them away.

"Hold on. Stop. Start from the beginning, and don't stop until you're done." She crossed her arms and stared at him. He sighed and finished putting the cold items away before turning to her and telling her the entire story.

"What are you going to do? I mean, about work? Can she get you in trouble?" Dawn rubbed her arms. "Why would she do that? Make trouble for you? If she's looking for support, putting your job in jeopardy is stupid."

"I don't think she has a firm grasp on reality. Right now, I'm more worried about the baby, even if it's not mine." Blay rubbed the back of his neck. "Dad's looking into what can be done. Maybe we can have her committed or something, but she hasn't done anything to endanger herself or anyone else..."

"That we know of." Dawn finished the sentence for him. She moved toward the grocery bags more out of habit than anything. "How is your mom handling it?" She took out a couple of lemons and a small bag of rice.

"She was pissed at being out of the loop, of course, and then she wanted to know what I was going to do if the baby is mine." He grabbed the asparagus and took it to the fridge.

Dawn batted his words away with a swipe of her hand in the air. "Well, that's an obvious answer. You're going to love it and give it a good home."

"She was concerned you'd dump me because of

the complication of a baby." He wasn't looking at her when he spoke, so she waited for him to turn to face her.

"First, it's not your momma's place to worry about that. This thing between us is between you and me, and I have no problem telling her that, but I get her concern. Look, I've helped raise a baby. It isn't easy. It's damn hard. I don't know where we're going as a couple, but I know I want to stick it out and see. The drama surrounding Ellen hurts you, so it hurts me. How could it not? When Ellen has that baby, we'll find out if she's yours, and we'll make decisions then. Yes, we need to be prepared for the possibility, and we can have lots of long, hard conversations, but I'm not bailing on what we're becoming because of a possibility. Hell, if I'm honest, I don't see myself bailing if this becomes a reality."

Blay stared at her for a moment. "She?"

Dawn blinked at him. "What?"

"You called the baby 'she'." He reached out and pulled her toward him, and she went willingly.

"Blay, I'm worried you inhaled too much smoke during the last three shifts. Didn't you hear anything else I said?" Dawn squinted at him and reached up and placed her hands on his cheeks, keeping his eyes on hers.

He nodded. "I heard you're not bailing on me. You're not afraid to tell my mother off, that you hate it when Ellen acts out, and that you want a girl." He dropped down and kissed her. She molded into his body.

The kiss wasn't meant to stoke passion, but it did. He didn't move his hands to excite her body, yet just the feel of his embrace and soft kiss quickened her pulse and stirred her desire. This man wrecked her in the best possible way. The entirety of Blayze King filled her to overflowing. There wasn't a part of him, even those parts that included his past, that could chase her away. She loved all of him. It was him, not the dream of something more, not the desire for things in the future, but today, yesterday, and all the nights before, she'd become immersed in the man she adored. He ended the kiss, and just above her lips, he spoke again. "That's why I'm in love with you."

She opened her eyes and stared into his. In those ice blue depths, she saw and felt the truth of his words. Her hands shook as she opened her soul to him. "I love you, too."

Her phone ringing in her purse made her jump, and that startled Blay. Humor lanced the flood of emotions. Laughing, she grabbed her purse and dug around for her phone. She swiped it, answering, "This is Dawn."

When no one answered, she spoke again. "Hello, this is Dawn. Can I help you?"

"You can die." The woman's voice pierced the silence, and then the call was gone. She dropped the phone from her ear and stared at the blank screen. Had she imagined that or had someone actually said those words? She blinked and lifted her eyes to Blay.

"What is it? What's wrong?"

She dropped the phone. "It's probably nothing, but those phone calls I've been getting have always been a nuisance. So, I block them when they get to be a pain, and the next day, I get another one from a different number. Tit for tat. It's pretty common when you're the ax the boss uses to fire people."

Blay moved over and picked up the phone. "This wasn't a hang-up, was it?"

She shook her head. "When I asked if I could help them, she said I could die."

"What?" Blay handed her the phone she'd just set down. "Let me in to see the number, please."

She entered her code and handed it to him. "Why do you want to see the number?" He took out his phone and pulled up Ellen's number. They compared the digits.

"Not even the same area code."

Blay nodded and relaxed a bit. "You need to let Clyde know about this. There is a line that human decency doesn't go past, and those ex-employees have been stomping the hell out of it. Death threats are nothing to trifle with. The next time this phone rings and you don't know who it is, let me answer, please?"

She put her hands on her hips. "You think that will matter? Seriously, the day of the caveman is long gone. I can handle my own business."

"Babe, I never doubted that for a minute. You're smarter than I ever could be, but this is a matter of safety, and there is safety in numbers. I think if they know you have someone else here, they might think twice about calling you again." Blay pulled her in and held her against him. She held tight to the anger brewing inside her. Those employees were stepping over a line. He held her and rocked side to side as they clung to each other. She took the time to process the sparse ten minutes that she'd been home. Finally, she nodded. "You're right."

He chuckled. "Of course, I am, but which instance are we talking about, specifically?"

"Those employees we fired have gone too far. I'll talk to Clyde, and I'll make a police report on it in the morning. But right now, I need to change clothes while you put the groceries away, or it will be midnight before we eat." She pulled back and looked up at him.

He smiled and kissed her. "Your wish is my command."

She picked up her heels and laughed, "Well, thank you, Genie. Could you pour me a glass of wine, too?"

"Done," he called as she padded down the hallway. She put her clothes in the laundry and shrugged into an oversized T-shirt and a pair of yoga pants. She passed by her dresser and frowned. The picture of her and Gage was in the wrong place. She stopped and looked around the room. *Whatever.* She must have hit it this morning on the way out the door. That or her mind was working overtime thanks to Ellen and her disgruntled ex-employees.

As she padded back into the kitchen, Blay asked, "What did the woman do at the warehouse to get her fired?"

"Which one? We let two go. One was a dispatcher, and one was a warehouse worker. Both were taking things that didn't belong to them. Stealing from Clyde is a guaranteed way to get yourself fired." She picked up the glass of wine he'd poured for her and took a sip. "So, you never did tell me about your shifts. How did things go?"

Blay shrugged. "When you don't work with your team, it's different. The inside jokes go over your head, and people tend to be overly direct when you respond, but Bailey needed the time, so when he asked, it was a no-brainer. Oh, he sent me a picture of his kid. It's in my text messages."

Dawn walked over and swiped his phone. Blay didn't lock his, which she thought was ridiculous. "Wow, look at that head of hair." The baby's hair was just as dark as his mom and dad's. "They are a beautiful family."

"Yeah, they're pretty happy, too. Bailey said he was thrilled to be sleep-deprived. They've been trying to have kids forever. Finally, they saved up enough money to do fertility treatments. He said he was happy for just one baby, but he was kinda hoping for a multiple so Tanya didn't have to go through the treatments again." Blay retrieved the chicken. "What are we making?"

"Panko-crusted chicken breasts with lemon cream sauce, asparagus, and jasmine rice."

Blay's stomach made a loud rumbling noise of agreement. "Sorry, I was going to stop for a sandwich when Mom called. It's been a day."

"For both of us, it would seem. Go get yourself a snack and a beer, and I'll get things started."

"Deal." He kissed her and headed to the fridge.

His phone vibrated on the counter. She slid over and glanced at the screen. "Ellen's calling. Can I answer it?"

"Do we want to add gasoline to the fire? Let it go to voicemail." Blay popped the top of his beer and threw the cap away.

She turned and stared at him. "What was it you said? There's safety in numbers, and if she knows there is someone else here, maybe she'd think twice about calling you?"

"Ouch, my own words used against me. Vicious, aren't you?" Blay handed her the phone.

She smirked at him. "You have no idea." Swiping the face, she put the phone to her ear. "Hello?"

There was silence on the other end. "Hey, Ellen? This is Dawn. I'm with Blay, his girlfriend. I know all about you and the baby, and I'm not going anywhere. Oh, and trying to get him in trouble at work and dropping by at the home front was also a big mistake. If you're trying to find support, you're going about it all wrong." She glanced at Blay. He leaned closer, and she moved the phone away from her ear. They waited for ten or fifteen seconds. The only thing she heard was heavy breathing. "Guess you have nothing to say. You take care, okay? Goodbye." Dawn swiped the face of the phone to end the call. She reached for her wine and took a sip.

"You're fearless, you know that?"

She laughed. "Oh, no, I fear a lot of things, but fools and fuck-ups are my job. I've been Clyde's hatchet for a long time. I never make it personal. I simply point out the facts. This is what transpired, and this is the result. She can't hate me for stating facts. Well, she can, but I didn't do anything to poke the bear; I just told the truth."

He turned off the burner she'd just turned on. "How about we make dinner tomorrow night? Tonight, we can order in."

She slipped her arms around his neck when he pulled her into him. "Whatever will we do while we wait for dinner to arrive?"

"Oh, I have a few ideas." He leaned down and kissed her neck, moving from the hollow near her shoulder up toward her ear. His hands slipped under her t-shirt and traveled her body, igniting a slow-burning desire that would consume them in a whirlwind of desire. "I'll call in an order and meet you in the bedroom."

Slowly, she pulled away from him and stepped

backward. She waited until she cleared the view of the kitchen window before she pulled the shirt over her head and dropped it on the floor. Blay's growl did little to stop the shimmy out of her yoga pants. Naked, she pulled the scrunchie out of her hair and let it drop to her shoulders. Blay slapped his phone on the counter and started walking toward her. She backed up as he advanced. There was no game here; she wanted to be caught, and he wanted to catch her.

Blay crashed into her at the door to her bedroom. Sweeping her up in his heavily muscled arms, she was on the bed the next instant. She shimmied into the middle as he undressed. She stayed up on her elbows and let her legs open just a bit as she watched him. God, he was fierce, the sharp relief of his muscles under his skin shifted as he moved. He opened the drawer and grabbed a condom.

"You don't need that any longer." She'd been on the pill for over a month now. They were protected.

"Thank God. I'm starving for you." He growled the words as he lowered. She wrapped her arms around his neck and pulled him to her. The feel of his body against hers ignited that smoldering flame she carried for him into a blazing inferno. She opened her legs so he could settle between them. Their sex ran the gambit from 'sweet and slow' to 'I want you right now'. Tonight crashed through want to need. Blay lifted her leg and centered himself. He covered her mouth with his and entered her with one hard thrust. She arched into him, needing more. He adjusted his position and lifted onto his knees, dropping onto straight arms above her. He flicked his hips, and she gasped.

Damn, how did he do that to her? Sparks flitted through her core, and when he thrust again, they multiplied. She grabbed his biceps and held on. He rolled his hips and quickened his pace. She stared up at him and gasped when he pushed a bit harder.

"Like that?" He leaned down and kissed her.

"God, yeah. Don't stop." She wrapped her legs around his.

He dropped to his elbows and slid his arms under her shoulders. "Not until I send you to heaven." He lowered for another kiss as his hips moved in a delicious ebb and flow. The connection between them became the center of her world, and the rest of her life's worries slipped away. Blay made love to her, and she returned that emotion in every touch and kiss. The man had become her touchstone. As she climaxed, her body clenched rhythmically, sending the most beautiful sensations through her. She held onto his muscular body as he hilted inside her and found his release.

He flopped to his side, pulled her to him, and kissed the top of her head. "I love you." He whispered the words reverently.

She tilted her head back and stared up at him. "I love you, too." When his lips descended to hers, she closed her eyes. She was in love for the first time in her life. The enormity of the emotion threatened to swallow her, sending a small jolt of fear through her. He lifted away and smiled down at her. Her heart shifted, sending all doubt skittering away. She smiled up at him. Being consumed by this man wasn't a bad thing.

Not at all.

CHAPTER 9

Studying for the engineer exam deserved his undivided attention, and when he studied, everything but the station house's alarm faded into the background. It had taken a lot to get the recommendations to go for the promotion, and the Lieutenant and crew were behind him, even if it meant he'd be transferred to another station house. But the raise in pay and the risk reduction were worth the effort and the change. He'd worked up from attack hose to entry team, and he'd proven his worth on his crew. That earned him respect and the chance to move up. He flipped through his notes and looked at the training material on the newest pumping system for one of the largest tankers the city owned. It would be sweet to slide into one of the fleet's banner engines, but as long as he made engineer, he'd be happy in any engine.

A knock behind him jarred him from his studies. He spun and stood up. "Yes, sir?" The Lieutenant stood in the doorway.

"I talked with the Battalion Chief. He filled me in on what is happening." Lieutenant Rocker strolled into the communal room the crew used for studying or computer-based training.

Blay sighed and rubbed the back of his neck. "He said he'd tell you what was going on. That's why I didn't say anything earlier."

"I get it. This woman, has she done anything that would lead you to believe she's a danger to herself or others?" The Lieutenant motioned to the chair Blay'd recently vacated.

Blay sat down, and Rocker pulled over another chair. "Sir, she's been a nuisance, and if she could make trouble for me, then yeah, I think she'd do that. The visit to my mom and seeing the BC here at the station were completely unexpected. Would she hurt herself? I don't think so because she might lose the leverage she has over me if she did. Others? I can't answer the question because I don't know."

"The BC said you didn't know if the child is even yours." Rocker leaned forward on his elbows.

"No, sir. The first thing I did was to ask for a paternity test. She's refused. Until I know for sure that she's carrying my child, I'm keeping clear of her. I've contacted the private investigator I used at the beginning of this situation. I want to know who she is and her background. The only thing I asked him to do earlier was to make sure she was pregnant and not phishing me for some reason. He was able to confirm she was pregnant, but nothing else. She doesn't live where I met her when she told me she thought I was the dad. She used a different address at the doctor's office, which is a vacant apartment for which there is no forwarding address."

Rocker nodded. "Years ago, when there wasn't as much grey in my hair, a lady claimed that I was the father of her child. I'd been married for three years, and I never strayed. Never wanted to if you know what I mean. This woman went as far as to put my name on the birth certificate. I had to hire a lawyer and contest the affidavit that she signed. I hired a private investigator and found out the woman had also tried this with her previous child. By the time I had proof that the child wasn't mine, my wife had left me. Don't get behind the eight-ball on this one, King. Hire a lawyer and get the court moving sooner rather than later."

Blay stared at his Lieutenant. "Did you ever get back with your wife?"

"No, but two years later, I met and married LaDonya. She's my world, so maybe things happen for a reason. But take it from someone who has been down that road: get in front of it."

"Thank you." He stood and extended his hand when his Lieutenant rose from his chair.

"You can thank me by acing that test."

"That's the goal, sir."

"When do you take it?"

"Three weeks."

"Yeah, and then you wait three months to see where you rack and stack. I know that waiting. It sucks."

"Like waiting to see if you're on the Captains list." He jabbed fun at his Lieutenant. The man was damn good and up for promotion to captain.

"Just like that." Blay watched Rocker leave and then grabbed his phone. His brother Brock was friends with a district attorney. Maybe he could recommend a good lawyer. He tapped in the text and hit send. An alarm in the background sounded. He waited to hear his unit called, but the response was for the medical team. He pocketed the phone and found where he'd stopped in his notes. He was in the review phase of his training. His mind was full of troubleshooting and systems, pressures, and quick response actions should a system fail. He pulled his index cards forward, and with the documentation on the computer and the information he'd outlined, he'd developed flash cards he could take with him and study when he had a moment.

His phone vibrated about thirty minutes later. Expecting a text from Brock, he glanced at the face. He smiled and grabbed the phone. "Hey, you, what's up?"

"I didn't catch you at a bad time, did I?" Dawn asked.

"I don't answer my phone if I'm actively fighting a fire." He laughed when she mimicked him.

"Funny, King. Seriously, can you talk for a second?"

"Sure, what's up?"

"Clyde's bank approved the merger we've been working on. He wants to go out and celebrate tomorrow night. Would you like to be my plus-one?"

Her plus-one was where he belonged, and the answer was a no-brainer. "I'd love to. Where and when?"

"Can you meet us here at the office at six-thirty?

I'll bring a change of clothes. It's just easier than fighting traffic to the house and back."

"I can. What's the dress code?"

"We're going to Drago, so sport coat at a minimum."

Blay whistled, "Your boss is pulling out all the stops. That's a ritzy place."

"His husband Paul is part owner, so he has an in," Dawn laughed and then sighed contentedly. "They're very curious about you."

He laughed, "Should I be worried?"

"Nah, I think the firefighter in you can handle the inquisition that comes with being my boyfriend."

The last word was said quietly, and it made him feel ten feet tall and fireproof. A sudden thought popped into his head. "Really? Have you seen this inquisition before?" For the first time in his life, that green monster called jealousy that he'd heard his brothers talk about crept up onto his shoulder and plopped his hairy butt down. He tried to play it off, but damn, that little guy jabbed him hard and deep with his claws.

"Nope. You'll be the first, but I have faith in your internal fortitude," Dawn chuckled.

"What are you doing tonight?" He glanced at the clock. "Wine and a book?"

"No, actually, I'm staying late again. Clyde is hosting three back-to-back meetings next week, and we're all scrambling to make sure everything is done. First, he's bringing in all the unions to set up a schedule for collective bargaining agreements. Then we have the logistics showcase to prep for and meetings with his lawyers and accountants after that. Finally, he's thinking of going public but wanted to run the pros and cons. You didn't hear that from me, by the way. That would be insider information."

"My lips are sealed. Don't stay too long and call me when you get home. Is anyone there with you?"

"Yep. This place has people coming and going at all hours, but now we have a keycard access system. The truck the boss let me use is right outside in his private parking space. He's put in an order for a reserved parking sign for me, too, so when I get my car back, I'll be under the bright lights and in view of the new surveillance system he's putting in."

"I'm glad he is taking steps to protect you."

"I don't need protection. My car does." She giggled at her joke.

"I beg to differ; you are much more important than your car." The klaxon bleated, drowning out anything she would have said. "Got to go. Call me on your way home. Love you." He spit the words out after the alarm silenced.

"Love you, too. Be safe."

He was moving as he dropped his cell into his pocket. The doors to the station were rolling up as he hit the engine and kicked off his tennis shoes. He toed into his boots and pulled up the suspenders of his turnout gear. Hefting himself up into his seat, he slipped the seatbelt on and put on his headgear.

When they pulled up to the scene, he dropped down with his turnout coat and helmet on. Royal and he moved to the first car. A woman had a nasty gash to her head from a sideways blow. Her vehicle didn't have side-impact airbags. Royal worked on her as Blay moved to the next car.

The medical team responded, driving up after them. They took the next car and moved fast to protect the person pinned in the car while the rest of his crew put out the fire that had consumed the engine compartment.

He moved up to the front car. It was halfway under a semitruck's trailer. A police officer was bending over, talking to the driver. He looked up, and his eyes told Blay to hurry. "Here is the fire department. They'll get you and your wife out."

Blay crouched down and took a look. *Damn.*

"My wife, she's not talking." The man behind the wheel wheezed the words. The steering wheel was impaled against the guy's chest. His legs were somewhere in the mangled mess below the dash.

"Don't worry. We'll take care of her and you. What's your name?"

"Duane."

"Okay, Duane, we're going to work to get you out of here." He grabbed his radio and relayed the information using the ten series codes, clear and concise instructions alerting the others to the emergency he had.

His transmissions were acknowledged immediately. Within ten seconds, Lieutenant Rocker was on the scene as well as the senior EMT, Dorsey. The woman wasn't conscious. The amount of twisted metal that filled the vehicle's interior prevented any extensive examination of anything but Duane's exposed body parts. The Lieutenant radioed for another medical team to respond, and Royal joined him. With the fire out, the rest of his crew stayed with the other injured parties until the ambulances arrived.

The Jaws of Life and a saw with a unique hybrid chain-wrapped blade appeared, and he and Royal prepped the man as well as they could. Any damage

KRIS MICHAELS

to his legs would be unknown until they could lift the dash off the man. The senior EMT draped a tarp between Duane and his wife. "What are you doing?" Duane's strangled cry escaped.

"It's okay. We don't want anything from over here to get over there. Duane, we're going to cut the roof off, and there will be sparks. I'm going to put a barrier over you, too." He didn't know if the woman would make it, but his priority was getting this guy out so the ambulance crew could work on him.

Blay held the barrier over both him and Duane as the crew used the rotary saw to cut the roof's rear posts and a line in the metal near the semi-truck. Blay kept checking on Duane. When the roof was lifted off, he moved out of the way for the jaws of life. They started on the driver's side, which told him the wife was either in better condition than Duane or she was beyond help.

As they inserted the hydraulic jaws to pry apart the vehicle, Duane looked at him and gasped, "Do you love someone?"

"I do," Blay responded without hesitation.

"Take care of them, son. My Missy isn't alive, is she?"

Blay glanced at the tarp that hadn't lowered. "They're still working with her."

144

Duane's brow unwrinkled, and he wheezed, "No. She's right there. I need to go." The man's eyes fixed past his shoulder.

Blay glanced back. Nothing but a bridge guard. He turned around. Duane's eyes no longer focused but stared unseeingly.

Blay went into action. He and the team followed every protocol and pulled Duane from the wreckage seconds later. The ambulance EMTs took over. After he was relieved and had passed the information he knew, he walked over to the other side of the car.

"She's gone. Died within minutes, I'd say." Their lead EMT, Keith Fontana, motioned to the piece of metal that practically cut the woman in half at the hips. Her clothes and the metal itself had prevented him or Duane from seeing the extent of her injuries. Blay glanced back at the spot where Duane had said he'd seen his wife. A shiver passed over him. He looked back toward where the medics were trying to resuscitate Duane. A handful of minutes with the man had seared a desire into his soul. That kind of love, the type of love that bound you to the person you loved both on earth and beyond—*that* was the type of love he wanted to build with Dawn.

CHAPTER 10

Dawn yawned as she got into the truck. She'd worked far longer than she'd initially planned, but with the office quiet and the phones not ringing, she was able to work up a strawman schedule for all three of the meetings and email them to Clyde. She also went through about two hundred emails that had been on the back burner and cleared out her inbox. The ones she needed to work on were flagged, and she'd added each item to her calendar with a link to the email. She was also in the hiring process for a corporate HR specialist. She and Clyde'd had a three-hour meeting and outlined what responsibilities he wanted her to retain, those she could farm out, and which ones needed a specialist. HR was one of those specialties. As she moved forward, Clyde wanted her to learn more about the operational side of the business and move into a management role with him. With work on solid ground and her relationship with Blay blooming, she found herself content in a way she'd never thought possible.

She smiled and keyed in a text to Blay, letting him know she was on her way home. The trip home, for the most part, was muscle memory. There was little traffic at nine-thirty. As she passed through the intersection where Brody had almost been killed years ago, she still said a thanks-filled prayer that her sister's husband had been saved, even if that accident had put a myriad of issues into place that the couple had to overcome.

Dawn slowed as she turned the corner of her street. Several fire engines blocked the way. She pulled over and got out of the truck. Her feet dragged on the blacktop as she tried to comprehend what had...

"Oh, my God! That's my house!" She dropped her purse and sprinted toward the burned-out shell. A cop caught her around the waist and lifted her off the ground. "Put me down! That's my house!"

The guy put her down but stood in front of her.

"It isn't safe right now. Come with me. We'll get you in as soon as we can."

Dawn let herself be steered away from her house. "Wait, my purse. I dropped my purse." She yanked her elbow out of the police officer's grip and backtracked. The contents of her purse were scattered over the street.

"I saw someone try to steal it." Mrs. Klein, her neighbor, shuffled up in her housecoat and slippers. "I shouted at them and flashed them with my laser pointer." She jiggled the red light on the street as she talked.

Dawn nodded, acknowledging her neighbor's comments. She stared at the odd assortment of stuff she had in her purse before she went to her knees and started to pick it up. Mrs. Klein bent down and offered her a handkerchief. "Aw, honey, I'm so sorry."

Dawn lifted her head, only then realizing she was crying. She waved off the hanky and swiped at her eyes, shoving everything back into her purse.

"The fire was huge before I saw it. I called 911, but so did Gloria. She was coming home from her daughter's play at school."

Dawn nodded, on some level understanding she needed to respond, but... She glanced through the tangle of vehicles toward her home. All the memories of her mom and dad, of Gage growing up. She closed her eyes tightly, releasing a new stream down her cheeks. The wall where they'd marked how tall Gage was each year on his birthday was gone, the photos of her parents, the family Bible and just... everything gone. Her life had gone up in smoke. She dropped to her butt and let the tears fall.

Mrs. Klein shuffled her old body next to her and hugged her. "I know you're hurting, honey, but you're fine. You're young. You'll be okay." The woman rocked her back and forth until she could control herself.

She sat up and dabbed at her tear-stained face with the handkerchief that she'd somehow ended up with and lifted her eyes to the house again. The firemen were milling around, putting away hoses and returning equipment to the engine. She stood and helped Mrs. Klein back to her feet. "Thank you, I just needed..." Hell, she didn't know what she needed.

"You needed to mourn, and you'll do that again. Each time it will get easier. Take it from an old woman who has lost more than most. Surviving isn't easy, but it is what makes us strong. It looks like that policeman wants to see you."

Dawn glanced over and nodded at the same

officer who had attempted to escort her away. She nodded at him and bent to kiss Mrs. Klein on the cheek. "Thank you."

The older woman cupped her face with a bony hand. "If you need a place to stay, my door is always open to you."

Dawn hugged the old woman lightly and pointed to the officer. "I'm going to go take care of business. Thank you for the generous offer, but I have somewhere I can go."

She waited until Mrs. Klein had made it back into her yard before she stepped over to the officer. "I'm sorry, it was such a gut punch."

The man nodded. "I understand. Let's go over here. As you can imagine, we have some questions."

Dawn nodded. "Of course." She followed the man and gave them a detailed rundown of her day after providing them with her name and telephone number. The address was a moot point. "You don't think I burned my own house down, do you?"

"We just have to cover all the bases, ma'am." The officer smiled nicely, but it didn't reach his eyes.

Wow... She'd said it as a joke. *But holy hell, the guy isn't laughing.*

"The arson investigator is in there now."

"Arson?" She squeaked the word.

"Yes, ma'am. The fire chief said his team found evidence that could be considered arson."

"Oh, my God. Who would want to... why?" She turned to stare at the walls that still stood, supporting a sagging roof. "Everything I owned was in there. Everything. Why would anyone do that?"

"That's what I'm going to find out, Dawn." A familiar voice whipped her attention in the other direction.

"Sean!" She let the man envelop her in a hug. "Why would someone do this to my home?"

Sean McBride released her from the hug but kept his arm around her shoulders. "I'm going to ask some obvious questions. Do you have any enemies?"

"So, you think it's arson?"

"Well, I have to wait for the lab results to come back, but someone doused the inside of your house with accelerant and started the fire. The concerning part is both the front and back door were locked when the department arrived."

"How is that possible?" She blinked and then looked at the once-brightly painted planter in front of the house. "Is the key still under the big planter?"

Sean nodded his head, and another man she hadn't noticed jogged over to the house and, after putting on blue gloves, lifted the pots one at a time.

KRIS MICHAELS

He shook his head. "I leave it there for Amber." She shivered and rubbed her arms, cold even in the warmth of the nighttime spring air.

"All right, we'll keep looking for it. What about anyone who would hurt you?"

She rubbed her arms harder. "I recently fired five people. My car was keyed, tires slashed. I've been getting hang-up calls at work and on my cell phone." She shivered again. "Is it cold?"

Sean took off his suit jacket and wrapped it around her shoulders. "Have you made a police report about the harassment?"

"No. I mean yes. My boss reported my car being vandalized because it happened on company property. The calls weren't bad until..." She pulled the jacket tighter. "Three days ago, they said that I should die."

"And you didn't report it?"

"Well, no." Sean looked at her and lifted his eyebrows. She shivered harder. "Maybe I should have."

"Hindsight is always twenty-twenty. Have you called Blayze?"

She shook her head. "He's on shift tonight."

"And he's covered a thousand times for others. This time, someone can cover for him. You don't need to be alone tonight." Sean lifted his phone to his ear. "Brock, get ahold of Blay and get him to Dawn's house. A fire. Yeah, I think so. No, she's okay but shaken up." He said goodbye and dropped his phone into the pocket of his slacks. "It will take him some time to get here. In the meantime, let's get that number off your phone, along with the date and the time. I'll need to see the HR records for those people you fired and anything your boss has from the police on his report of vandalism."

She nodded numbly and fished around in her purse. The contents were jumbled, and it took her several minutes to locate her phone. Blay had called once, and it was ringing when she finally dragged it from the bottom of her cavernous purse.

She swiped the face and answered, "Hello."

"Babe, are you okay?" Blay almost shouted the question.

"Yeah, no. Not really. Someone burned down my house." Her words were as pathetic as her scrambled emotions. Once again, her burning, sore eyes filled with tears.

"I'm on my way. The Lieutenant is calling in someone to cover my shift. Who is there with you?"

"Sean." She looked up at the man who winked at her.

"May I speak to him, please?" At Blay's request, she held out the phone to Sean.

He took the phone and gave Blay the same information he'd given her. She stared at the house she'd grown up in and the home her parents had left to her when they died. She could see her mom planting flowers in the bed under the living room window. Her father's chair, where he'd read the paper during the summer evenings on the porch, was charred and pushed over on its side. She leaned against the police patrol car. As Sean talked to Blay, she wondered what type of person would stoop to such a horrible act. Even Blay's crazy stalker had her limits. Sure, she'd tried to cause trouble, but this... This was criminal. She straightened her back with resolve. When Sean found out who did this, she was going to press charges. No one should be able to destroy a person's life with a swipe of a match. No one.

Sean disconnected and handed her the phone. "I think he's just as shook up as you are."

"If I'd been home tonight instead of working late, maybe this wouldn't have happened." She turned to look at him, seeking his opinion.

He shook his head. "I don't know. Sometimes arson is an act of rage or revenge. Sometimes it is a well-planned out and scripted act."

"Which is this?" She turned back to the house that was now only illuminated by portable lighting units. She turned around and noticed the fire trucks had left. *Huh.* She hadn't even heard them leave.

"I have a lot more work to do before I can say for sure." Sean glanced around and lowered his voice. "I'm staying until Blay gets here, but I need to get back in and gather some more samples. Are you okay?"

She drew a deep breath and nodded. "I will be." Not today, maybe not even next week, but eventually, she'd be able to put this horrendous act into perspective.

"The police officer is going to be here all night. We're considering this an active crime scene, and until we see it during the day, it will need to be protected. Also, when we clear, you'll be allowed to come and retrieve anything that wasn't ruined by the smoke or the water. I'll give you a heads up when that is going to happen as soon as I know."

"Thank you, Sean. I know it's not your job to babysit me. Go do what you need to do." She took off his jacket and handed it back to him.

"Please, keep that and stay warm. When Blay gets here, you can put it in my car." He nodded toward the sedan parked half on and half off the sidewalk.

"Thank you." She shouldered back into the warm material.

"You're welcome. I've got to go back to work."

She nodded. "Find out who did this, will you?"

"I'm going to do my best." Sean gave her a half-smile and strode back toward the house.

She settled against the hood of the patrol car and watched the shadows of Sean and his partner working inside the house. A small portion of the roof fell in. She jumped to her feet, but Sean's partner exited the house and waved at the officer. "Expected, and we're fine." He spoke loudly so they could both hear him.

"I don't know how they can do that job. I would hate to go into a building destroyed by fire," the cop said and then glanced at her. "Sorry."

She gave a humorless laugh. "Believe me, I understand. What I don't get is the type of person that would do this." She mused the last part to herself.

The cop crossed his arms and sighed. "In this job, you see the best of people and the worst."

She nodded. "My boyfriend's brothers are police officers. His dad, too."

The guy cast her a glance. "Yeah? Would I know them?"

"Probably. Chauncey King is his dad."

The cop muttered something that sounded like a curse word, but Dawn spun away from him at the sound of squealing tires. Blayze's truck careened around the corner at breakneck speed. His tires screeched against the blacktop as he slammed on the brakes. His door flew open, and he was running toward her, still wearing his HCFD uniform.

She ran toward him, and he wrapped himself around her. She held onto him and let him take some of the weight off her shoulders. He rocked back and forth as she half-talked, half-cried while detailing everything that happened.

He kissed the top of her head and rubbed her back as she finally stilled. "I'm sorry. I'm not this person. I'm not a blithering idiot." She hiccupped and blew her nose with Mrs. Klein's kerchief that she still had wadded in her hand.

"Baby, everyone knows how strong you are. No one doubts that. Leaning on me doesn't make you weak." He brushed her ponytail with one hand while holding her close to him with the other. "Let's go to my place. We'll come back when they clear the scene."

"Sean said he'd let me know as soon as that happens." She leaned back. "He needs the information in my phone."

"I can take that for him, ma'am." The officer that she'd been talking to spoke, breaking the small bubble they'd formed.

Blay leaned down and kissed her. "Give me your keys, and I'll move Clyde's truck."

"In my purse, somewhere. It was scattered all over the street."

Blay paused his reach for her purse. "Why?"

"I dropped it when I saw this." She waved a hand at her home. "Mrs. Klein said that she thought someone was trying to take it, but her eyes aren't so good. You can knock on her door and ask if we can park the truck in her driveway tonight. I don't think I'm capable of concentrating on traffic."

"Can do." He began taking things out of her purse in search of the keys. "Are you sure you took the keys out of the ignition?" He rummaged through her purse as he spoke.

"Ah, no, not really." She glanced down the street to the truck.

"I'll go look and ask Mrs. Klein." He dropped a kiss on her lips before he strode down the street.

"That's Commissioner King's kid?"

"His youngest son, yes."

The guy nodded. "Let's start with the basics. What information did the detective want?"

The guy pulled out a notebook and started writing as she repeated the vandalism story and then pulled up the telephone call list, pinpointing the call from who she believed was one of her disgruntled ex-employees. She gave Clyde's name and contact information so Sean could reach him about the vandalism report. The HR records she could provide him, and she told the officer that, too.

Clyde's truck pulled into Mrs. Klein's drive, and she heard the horn beep as Blay locked it. He made his way back to them and waited as the officer asked more questions. She answered each, including when she left work and how she could vouch for her time at the office. Blay grunted at the question, but she'd had time to internalize the need to make sure she wasn't trying to rip off the insurance company or something. She detailed how she swiped in and out of the building, and only authorized people could gain access. Guests were now provided an escort. The place was far too large to leave them alone to ramble.

When he finally told her he was done, she was relieved. Blay walked with her to put Sean's jacket back in his car before he helped her into his truck. He started the engine and did a three-point turn, heading the truck away from her home. She didn't look back. There wasn't a need.

Her phone rang in her hand. Amber, her sister. She closed her eyes and answered the phone. After she finished talking to Amber, reassuring her that she was going to stay with Blay and that she'd see her in about a half-hour, she called Clyde.

He demanded she take the rest of the week off and informed her in no uncertain terms that he would find out who was responsible. She could hear Paul, Clyde's husband, in the background asking questions and getting more and more irritated as Clyde continued to ignore him. "Go tell Paul what's happening. Needless to say, dinner is off tomorrow. I only own the clothes I have on my back."

"I can open a line of credit for you," Clyde immediately offered.

"No, I can get what I need." She sighed as they turned onto the road where Blay's apartment building stood. "I've got to go, Clyde. I'll call as soon as I have any additional information."

"You better, or you'll have me to deal with," Clyde chided her. "Take care of yourself, Dawn."

"I will. Goodnight."

She dropped the phone and looked over at Blay, who hadn't said a word the entire trip. "I'm sorry."

His head snapped toward her. "For what?"

"Being a bother." She was so damn tired and, well… defeated.

He pulled into his parking slot and put the truck into park. "I love you. I was terrified for you, and now I'm angry for you, but what I will never be is bothered by anything you have going on in your life. This is something we will deal with together. We're a team now, Swanson. You're stuck with me."

She leaned over and dropped her head on his shoulder. "Hell of a lot to saddle you with so soon."

"I can carry the load." He wrapped his arm around her shoulder and hugged her. God, he could. He was a rock of strength and support.

The front door of the apartment flew open, and Amber raced out to the truck. "I think your sister wants to see you." Blay opened the driver's side door, and Amber jumped up on the step and reached over him, hugging her in the most awkward way possible.

"Stop, you're strangling me," she managed to laugh as she twisted toward her sister.

Amber released her and hit Blay. "Get out of my way."

He laughed, and when she moved, he slipped out, giving her the driver's seat. Dawn was immediately wrapped in her sister's arms. They talked forever and cried some, too. Dawn tracked Blay as he talked with Brody and then as he watched Gage take the dogs across the street for a play and comfort break. She and Amber clambered down from the truck. She moved into Blay's arms, and Amber slid into Brody's. Blay locked up his car, and they walked up the stairs together, following Gage, the dogs, Brody, and Amber. At Blay's apartment, Amber gave her another hug and then turned with her husband to walk up the next flight of stairs to their home.

The dogs pranced around them when they entered. She bent down and loved on each one of them. The simple act of giving a little love to the animals made her feel better, although exhaustion wrapped itself around her like a cocoon.

Blay took her into the bathroom. With gentleness and care, he helped her shower, gave her a t-shirt to sleep in, and pulled the covers up to her chin when she laid down. She watched him walk toward his side of the bed. She loved him so much.

It was her last waking thought.

CHAPTER 11

Blay prowled through his apartment, tired of trying to sleep. He'd grabbed a couple of hours of fitful rest, but the majority of the night he'd held Dawn while she slept. It was early, almost six, and he didn't want to wake her by banging around in the apartment, so he left a note, put on his running gear, and leashed the dogs. They slipped out the door, and instead of leaving it open, he locked it. Last night, what had happened had filled him with rage, and that was the emotion he was trying to work out of his system with a run. He walked the dogs across the street and let them sniff and take care of business before he called them back, leashed them, and they started on their run.

When Brock had called and told him what was

KRIS MICHAELS

happening, he'd freaked. His Lieutenant made him stop and repeat everything. Twice. The time it took to repeat what was happening and make intelligent conversation grounded him. Thank God. As soon as they knew a crew member was inbound, Rocker let him leave. Totally against policy, but family emergencies blurred lines, and Randy Crane, who was covering for him, lived less than three miles from the station.

His feet now hit the pavement in a soothing, repetitive beat. He concentrated on the in and out of his breath as he picked apart his thoughts and, yes, fears. Sean had promised he'd call this morning as soon as he had any information, but the fire was purposefully set from what his friend relayed yesterday. *Arson.* He sped up, and the dogs loped alongside him. A fucking asshole had destroyed Dawn's house and all her possessions. He hadn't gone into the house. He didn't need to. When he pulled up, he noticed the sagging line of the roof and the vents that firefighters had cut to access the fire through the attic. That little ranch was gutted. What the flames hadn't destroyed, the water from the response would have. She'd loved that house and had worked hard to keep it up. His heart broke for her, not only because he loved her but also because that

164

home was a piece of her past, a gift from her mom and dad.

He made another loop with the dogs before they walked to cool down. He opened the gate and let the dogs sniff in the lot he and Brody had purchased. Even though he was tired, they still had energy.

He heard the door to the apartment building close and glanced over his shoulder. Brody walked across the street carrying two cups of coffee. "Saw you leave for a run. I figured you were up almost all night. I know I would have been." He handed Blay a cup which he accepted gratefully.

"How do you do it? Amber works in a dangerous profession. After last night, I want to lock Dawn up so nothing can hurt her." Blay took a sip of the coffee and sighed.

"Well, first off, if either of us tried to lock up either of those women, we'd be castrated by said women." Brody chuckled and took a sip of his coffee.

Blay bobbled his head side to side. "True."

"We can only do our best. There was no way you or she knew this was coming. There was nothing you could have done to prevent it. Beating yourself up about it isn't going to help." Thor and Oden trotted over, and Blay gave each of them some love. "What do you have planned for today?"

"Well, I need to get with the Captain. I need to take some time off to help her. Shit, she's going to need everything."

"Amber has a stack of clothes sitting by the door. I'll bring them down when we go in. Plus, Mom has sent out a 911 call to all the girls."

"That's good." His mother was a bit of a busybody at times, but she was the best when it came to rallying people for a cause. He couldn't think of a better cause than taking care of Dawn. "I'm waiting on a call from Sean."

"Talked to him about five minutes ago. He was heading back into work but stopping at the lab first. He considers Dawn family, and he'll exhaust every avenue to find out who did this."

Blay took another drink of his coffee. "You and I both know the chances of that are slim to none."

Brody nodded as he watched the dogs. "For a normal run-of-the-mill random-type arson, true, but he was looking into the ex-employees. If they slaughtered her car, this isn't a big step. Could be that simple."

Blay didn't say anything because nothing about what happened yesterday was simple. He took another swig of his coffee and whistled for the dogs. They trotted over to him and sat as he hooked the leash to their collars. "Thanks for last night and for keeping Amber here until we cleared the scene."

"Man, let me tell you, that was a hard thing. Talk about one pissed woman, but she understood after I got her to listen to reason." Brody walked with him across the street. He held Brody's cup so he could unlock the door and let them all in. "I'll bring down those clothes and other bits that Amber has set aside for Dawn when I take Gage to school."

"Where's Amber?" He hadn't even noticed if her car was in the parking lot.

"She, Rayburn, and Watson are working a case, and she wasn't happy about leaving, but they're close to making a collar on a mid-level dealer."

Blay let go of the leashes, and the dogs walked up the stairs by themselves as he and Brody followed. "Which means they could roll him for the bigger guy."

"It is the dance we do," Brody agreed. "Oh, by the way, the family is congregating at yours tonight. Everyone wants to make sure Dawn is okay. So, restock on beer and wine." Brody slapped him on the back and turned the corner, walking up the stairs leading to his apartment.

Blay grunted an acknowledgment and let himself into the apartment. The heavenly scent of bacon greeted him as he opened the door. The dogs trotted in, and he heard Dawn talking baby talk to them in the kitchen. He turned the corner just in time to see her give them each a small piece of bacon. "You're spoiling them."

She turned and smiled at him. His t-shirt dropped to mid-thigh on her and looked damn good. "They had their run, so now they can have a treat."

He walked over to her and pulled her into a hug before he kissed her. "Good morning. Did I wake you?"

"Good morning to you, too. No. I woke up and started thinking about everything I have to do today. I need to call the insurance company. My policy and all my important documents are in the bank in a safety deposit box, but the key was in the house, so I need to get to the bank and somehow get them to let me in. Then I have to buy clothes. Oh, I put the stuff I was wearing in the washer. I hope that's okay." She pulled away and walked over to the stove. "Fried or scrambled?"

He shrugged. "Whichever you'd like."

She nodded and cracked four eggs into the frypan. "Would you set the table?"

"On it." He gathered the silverware, napkins, and salt and pepper and arranged them. "Sean is supposed to call this morning, and Amber has clothes set aside for you upstairs. Brody will bring them down when he takes Gage to school. Amber had to go into work."

"Yeah, she told me last night. When do you have to go back?"

"I'm calling in and asking for some time off. I have so much vacation time and have worked extra shifts for just about everyone at the station. It won't be a problem." Blay handed her a plate. She slid two eggs onto his plate, and he gave her the other to repeat the process, then carried the plates to the table after she put two pieces of bacon and a slice of toast on each.

"You don't have to take time off because of me." She didn't look at him as she spoke. Instead, she concentrated on her toast.

He reached over and put his hand over hers. "I know. I know you can do this by yourself, but here's the thing. You don't have to go through it alone. I want to be here for you to help make your life a bit easier. Let me."

She lifted her eyes to his. "What did I do to deserve someone like you?"

Blay smiled at her and winked. "After four hundred and fifty-seven times, you said yes. Finally."

Dawn laughed, which was just what he wanted her to do. He was going to help her get through today, and if he had his way, he'd help her through the rest of their lives.

The process at the bank to get into the safety deposit box wasn't onerous, but it was expensive. The fee for rekeying the box was astronomical, but they didn't have a choice.

With her insurance policies in hand, they made phone calls and then headed to the diner across the street from the precinct where Kallie worked. His brother and sister-in-law would try to break free for lunch, and Sean would be in the area, too, so they would be killing two birds with one stone.

Sean had called right after breakfast, but the lab hadn't finished with the samples yet. He suggested they meet up at the diner for lunch to get a preliminary copy of his report and results he could release.

"This is nice." Dawn motioned toward the shiny silver diner car.

"Food is good, too. The cops at the precinct keep

it busy. We aren't that far away from my station. We hit it up sometimes when we're too busy to cook. Casey, the owner, will box it up for us and keep it warm if we get called out on the way here."

"Kallie works over there?" She pointed to the three-story building across the street.

"Yep. Brock did too for a while, but he had to transfer out. They were both going a little crazy. He was overprotective, and she wasn't having it. It works better for both of them if neither knows the day-to-day events. They both know the dangers; they just didn't want to stare them in the eye all day every day."

"That makes sense. I couldn't watch you run into a burning building without having a heart attack." She slipped off her seatbelt when he parked. "Speaking of which, we need to ask Sean when I can go back inside my house."

He grabbed her hand. "Don't expect much. Fire and water do a lot of damage."

She squeezed his hand. "I know, but I want to see it, you know what I mean? For closure, maybe."

"I get it." He did. He also knew it was going to be an emotionally charged experience. "Let's grab a booth."

Blay guided Dawn through the densely populated entryway of the dining car. At least twelve people were waiting for booths to clear, but he had his eye on the booth at the back because Kallie waved at him, grabbing his attention. His sister-in-law and his brother Brock had already managed to score a table. As they approached, Kallie slid from the booth and met Dawn at the center of the aisle. Kallie hugged Dawn as Blayze shook his brother's hand.

They all piled into the booth. Kallie grabbed Dawn's hand. "I'm so sorry about your house. Have you heard anything from Sean?"

"That's why we're here." Dawn looked at Blay and gave a halfhearted smile. "We've been getting things together for the insurance company. Sean said that he could give us a preliminary police report soon. He was supposed to meet us here."

Kallie turned to look at Brock. "Did you know Sean was coming today?" Brock nodded. Kallie slapped him on the arm. "Why didn't you tell me?"

Brock rubbed his bicep and laughed. "When? I got here thirty seconds before Blay and Dawn walked through the door."

"You had thirty seconds," Kallie countered.

"Excuse me if I wanted to kiss my wife before I told her that my best friend was showing up for lunch." Brock leaned forward and kissed his wife again.

Blayze relaxed and stretched his arm over the back of the booth as he watched his brother and sister-in-law tease each other.

Dawn relaxed beside him and whispered, "When I woke up this morning, I knew I had to do the things that I could do to make myself feel in control of the situation. Unfortunately, there's not a whole lot of control. I feel like I'm floating on the current with no paddle and no life preserver." She looked up at him. "If it wasn't for you, I don't know what I would have done."

Blayze dropped his arm from where it rested on the cushion and pulled her into his side. He dropped a kiss on her lips as he heard Sean's greeting.

"Sorry I'm late." Sean McBride slid into the booth, crowding Brock into Kallie. Sean and Brock had been best friends since the Kings moved in next door to the McBrides eons ago. "On the way over here, the lab called to tell me the test results were in. I swung by to grab them. I didn't think you'd mind waiting a couple minutes." Sean pulled an envelope from the breast pocket of his suit jacket. "According to the lab, the accelerant was a mix of gasoline and kerosene." Sean flipped the report to Blayze.

Dawn grabbed the paperwork and opened the folded pieces. Blayze glanced down at the type of report he'd seen many times. The first half of the paper included specifics about the lab, the tests completed, and the protocols to which the lab adhered. He let Dawn read through the required language and waited until she flipped the page. In the first paragraph, lab technicians indicated the mix of gasoline and kerosene, although they used the names of the chemical components.

Dawn looked across the table. "So, this proves it was arson."

Sean nodded his head in agreement. "That's going to be my official finding. I've got the preliminary police report almost finished. I can email it to you so you have it electronically. Depending on your insurance company, an electronic copy should do."

"That would be perfect, thank you." She rattled off her email address, and Sean entered it into his phone.

Brock stopped a harried waiter and ordered five specials, not allowing anyone to order anything different or object. When Kallie gaped at him, he looked confused. "What? If we order anything else, it'll take forever. Sean, do you have any leads other than the accelerant?"

Sean glanced at Dawn and then at him before he answered Brock's question. "I've been by Dawn's work and talked to her boss. He believes the recent firings would have the most motive for revenge against her. He's filed a police report on the vandalism of her car and had a copy of it for me. Unfortunately, there hasn't been any follow-up on it as far as I can tell. Jordan and I will be calling in all of them today."

Kallie flagged down the waiter as he rushed by. "We need two coffees." She looked around the table. "What do you guys want to drink? My husband forgot to order anything."

Brock shrugged. "Food's important right now. I've had my fill of coffee today."

Kallie snapped her head in his direction and drawled, "Who are you, and what have you done with my husband?"

Brock laughed, "I think I've had at least six pots this morning. I've been doing paperwork all morning, so I've practically had a coffee IV inserted. I need food before I have any more caffeine."

Sean shook his head. "I never thought I'd see the day."

Blayze pulled out his phone. "Hold on. I'll alert the press. Brock King doesn't want coffee." Laughter floated around the table and relieved some of the tension. They ordered their drinks and the conversation reverted to any leads Sean might have on finding the arsonist. The waiter returned with five open-faced roast beef sandwiches, each with a heaping serving of mashed potatoes, gravy, and mixed vegetables. Blayze tucked into the meal, as did the others. Conversation stilted a bit until their stomachs started to fill.

Kallie pointed her fork at Sean. "You know, you shouldn't keyhole your search to just the employees."

Sean lifted his eyes from his plate and narrowed his gaze at her. "What do you mean?"

"What about Blay's stalker?" Kallie placed her fork on her plate and lifted her coffee cup. "I have some personal experience with stalkers. They don't always go after the person they're fixated on. Could his supposed baby momma be a person of interest?"

Dawn put her fork down, too. "She's over five months pregnant. I'm sure one of my neighbors would have told me if a pregnant woman had walked up to my front door. Wouldn't they?" She looked at Sean.

"We're going back and talking to the neighbors today. We're also looking for any camera footage of people around your house from wi-fi camera doorbells. Everybody has them now. But not everybody has storage in the cloud."

"I didn't say she was the one to actually start the fire. But as we all know, she's manipulative and wants a relationship with Blay. So, I don't think it's a far stretch that she could cause trouble for Dawn." Kallie took a drink of her coffee.

"Arsonists have regimented motives, even though it is one of the hardest crimes to convict. We do know that the exact psychological determinants of people who set fires have variables. Still, according to most studies, a common thread in the majority of not-for-profit arsons is revenge." Sean scooped a heaping forkful of mashed potatoes up. "The first thing we look for is vengeance against the owner of the property. Then we ascertain if there are any enemies, if there are scorned lovers—"

Kallie smacked the table with her open palm, bouncing the plates and utensils. "Scorned lover! My point exactly. This woman wants Blay, and she can't have him."

The booths around them quieted, and heads turned. Brock covered Kallie's hand with his. "Calm down and let Sean finish, dear."

Kallie scrunched her nose at her husband. "You

were saying?" She turned and blinked rapidly as she spoke in an overly sweet tone.

Sean laughed. "I love her. You know that, right?"

Brock growled. "You got your own woman. She's mine."

Sean's belly laugh filled the air. "Whatever. Anyway, there are a couple of other motives. The heroic endeavor is basically a first responder who sets the fire to become the hero." Sean glanced at Blay.

Blay rolled his eyes and said a few not-so-nice mental curses. "I've spent my entire adult life learning how to put out fires. It makes me sick to think that anybody in our professions could start one."

Dawn put her hand on his thigh and squeezed it gently before she asked Sean, "What was the other type? You said there were a couple of other reasons?"

Sean's face reddened. "There are the rare few who take a perverse sexual pleasure in starting fires."

"Eww." Dawn made a face and then gave an exaggerated shiver. "But why? Other than the sexual thing. I don't want to know about that."

There was a rumble of chuckles around the table. Sean leaned forward, pushing his almost-empty plate out of the way. "Well, as I said, revenge or jealousy, insurance fraud, intimidation, to conceal a crime, or to throw the police off the trail of the crime, and of course, there's always the psychiatric afflictions. Things like pyromania, alcoholism, drug use."

"Dude, I don't know how you deal with these types of people on a day-to-day basis." Blay shook his head and leaned back away from his finished meal.

Sean snorted. "And I don't know how you run into a burning building. You must be feebleminded. Your mom or dad had to have dropped you."

Brock lifted his hand. "I dropped him two, no, three times."

Blay threw a wadded-up napkin at his brother before he circled back to Kallie's idea of Ellen being a suspect. "All joking aside, I don't think Ellen would do anything to hurt someone. I've never seen anything like that in her nature. But, again, I don't know her that well."

"Still, it's an avenue I think we need to explore. Kallie was right. We can't pigeonhole our investigation and fail to look at the bigger picture. I'm going to need all the information you have on her."

Blay pulled out his phone. "I have a document. I put this together after my lieutenant told me to get ahead of the situation. It has everything I can remember about meeting her both times. Her phone number, her physical description, and the address where I met her upstate when she told me she was pregnant. I'm also keeping a running total of emails, texts, and phone calls. I'll send you that in the email. Your personal one okay?"

"Perfect." Sean pulled out his phone. Blay sent it, and Sean flashed the screen when it showed up.

Dawn pushed her plate away. "She hasn't called since you told her you had a restraining order, has she?"

Blay shook his head. "No, but the texts and emails have doubled. Although, she hasn't shown up at Mom and Dad's again, nor has she shown up at work. As far as I'm concerned, that's a win. At least you'll never have to talk to her again."

Brock, Kallie, and Sean exchanged quizzical looks before Sean asked, "Dawn, you talked to Ellen?"

Dawn shrugged. "I talked. She listened."

Blay could see the concern in his brother's eyes, so he explained. "She answered my phone and told Ellen that she was my girlfriend and that going to my place of work and by our family home wasn't smart and it wasn't garnering any sympathy for her situation."

Brock glanced at Sean. "That could have been a trigger."

Sean nodded. "A lot of supposition, but I agree, it should be checked out. And with that, I need to go. Brock, thank you for lunch." Sean winked across the table at them and stood up.

"What? No, it's your turn," Brock sputtered as Sean darted down the aisle. "Damn it. He did it again." Brock pushed his empty plate toward the center of the table. "That man owes me at least ten meals."

Kallie laughed and kissed her husband's cheek. "It's a good thing you don't keep track. I better go, too. We'll see you tonight?" She glanced across the table.

"Tonight?" Dawn turned to look at Blayze.

"Ah, the family is going to gather at the apartment. They all want to see you for themselves to make sure you're okay."

Dawn cocked her head at him. "And you didn't tell me this earlier because...?"

Brock barked out a laugh. "I love not being the only one in the doghouse. Come on, babe, I'll walk you back to your office."

Kallie slipped out of the booth with Brock. Her parting comment of, "Give him hell, sister," didn't help the look Dawn was giving him.

"I didn't want to stress you out?" He tried the answer on for size. It kinda fit. *Didn't it?*

"My stress meter is pegged. I don't think anything could make it worse. Come on. We need to go to the store. There's almost nothing in your fridge. Oh, and alcohol. I'm not surviving today without alcohol."

"Speaking of stressful situations, we need to reschedule the meet with your boss."

Dawn groaned and dropped her head back on the cushion of the banquet. "Not until I can make it through the day without wanting to sit in a corner and cry. Okay?"

"Deal. Until then, it's just family." He stood up and offered her his hand before realizing that Brock had stuck him with the check. "Son of a…" He picked up the ticket off the table and glanced toward the door. Brock's smile was the last thing he saw before the door shut.

"Don't whine. It's just family, remember?" Dawn shooed him away from the table so she could get out.

Blay rolled his shoulders and followed Dawn toward the register. *Yep, just family.* Figuring out how to pay back Brock was going to be fun.

CHAPTER 12

Overwhelmed would be an understatement. Dawn sat amongst gift bags, small boxes, and piles of new clothes. Each member of the McBride and King family that walked through the door of Blayze's apartment carried a gift of some kind. The women had conspired on the list of her needed items. She now had the basics of a wardrobe and cosmetics. Additionally, she had several pairs of shoes and a drawer full of lingerie.

Amber moved a pile of boxes and sat down beside her.

"How did you guys manage to do this on a workday?"

Amber shrugged. "When somebody is important

to you, you do what needs to be done. How are you doing today?"

Dawn found Blayze standing in the kitchen with his brothers and the McBride boys. As if he sensed her stare, he glanced over at her. She smiled at him as she answered her sister's question. "I'm not going to lie. It's been rough. Blay has been wonderful. We found out from Sean that it was arson."

Amber nodded. "So, they believe it was a disgruntled ex-employee?"

"Sean is looking into that angle, yes. Kallie insisted he not exclude Ellen from consideration. She was basing that on her ex-husband, who turned out to be a stalker."

"Oh, yes, that man was insane. Which, if you look at it rationally, Ellen isn't too far off that mark." Amber snorted and took a drink of her wine.

Tara McBride walked up and found a clean space on the floor to sit beside them. "What are you talking about?" She crossed her legs and took a sip of her wine.

Amber lifted her wine glass. "We're talking about Blay's crazy stalker."

"She's not a stalker." Dawn rolled her eyes at her sister's terminology.

Bekki, Caitlyn, Erin, and Brie followed Tara over. Boxes and bags were moved as the women found places to sit. Kallie followed with a bottle of wine and a bottle of bourbon. "We should probably eat soon."

Dawn extended her empty glass toward Kallie. It was filled immediately with wine. "Hannah said not to do anything for food. She and Sharon were bringing dinner."

Kallie poured herself another drink of bourbon. "Well, then I hope she'll hurry up. I'm starving."

Bekki turned around and looked into the kitchen. "Yo, Blay! Bring us some chips or crackers before Kallie gets grumpy."

Dawn watched as Brock opened up the pantry door and grabbed two bags of chips. He strolled over and handed one to his wife before he tossed the other onto the coffee table. He bent down and received a kiss from Kallie before he sauntered back into the kitchen.

"That man loves me." Kallie opened up her bag of chips and popped one into her mouth.

"Where's Sean?" Caitlyn looked around the crowded apartment.

"He and Harper are running late. She was at a fire scene. Sean said he was going to wait for her before they came over." Tara opened the chip bag and took a handful.

"Where are the kids?" Brie asked.

"With the grandparents," Amber and Tara answered at the same time.

"Perfect. Give us the scoop on you and Blay!" Bekki reached forward and grabbed some chips. She popped one into her mouth while wiggling her eyebrows.

Dawn rolled her eyes. "I'm so not going to give you any details."

Caitlyn snorted inelegantly. "I really wish Blay wasn't in a relationship."

Every head turned in her direction. Dawn blinked, not knowing how to respond to that comment. Amber was the first to speak. "Do you have something against my sister?"

Caitlyn froze with the chip halfway to her mouth and looked from woman to woman. "Oh, God, no. I mean with Blay in a relationship, that only leaves me for the mothers to set up. I overheard Mom talking to Hannah. I don't need them to set me up with anyone. Seriously, you guys need to run interference."

Bekki stole the chip from Caitlyn's hand. "Seriously, why aren't you going out with that track coach? He's hot."

Caitlyn took her chip back. "He's also in a committed relationship with a linebacker for the Hope City Marauders."

Dawn took a sip of her wine and listened as the women teased each other. She was part of this family, and not just because she was Amber's sister and Gage's aunt.

Her gaze once again found Blay. The man had been a touchstone today. Every time she felt over-whelmed or became mired in the emotions of losing her home, he was there. She'd never really thought about the implications of having someone surround you with love. She'd always been a strong, independent woman. Solving problems, taking care of business, going about life—it was all she knew. The new addition of having someone there for her when things became too much was a blessing.

Thor and Oden wandered over to the coffee table, subtly begging for human food. Instead, they received pets and scratches from each of the women. Oden sat down beside Dawn and laid his head on the arm of the couch. She stroked the wiry fur as she listened to the women talk.

There was a loud knock on the door, and it burst open. Gage and Colleen ran into the apartment with Hannah, Chauncey, Sharon, and Colm following them. Each of the adults had bags full of food. The enticing aroma of spicy Mexican food filled the apartment.

Dawn hurried over to help with food. Hannah caught her in a hug and rocked her back and forth. "Sweet girl. I'm so sorry. If you need anything, anything at all, you let me know."

Still hugging Hannah, Dawn whispered, "You've already done so much. Thank you so much for organizing this tonight."

Hannah pulled away a bit. "I'm assuming you'll stay here with Blay, right?"

She could feel her face turn a brilliant red. "Yes, ma'am, I was hoping to, unless..." She could feel Blay's presence behind her.

"She's staying with me, Mom." Blay wrapped an arm around her waist and pulled her back into him. "We're both adults and in a committed relationship. We don't need to hear a lecture."

Hannah blinked from Blay to Dawn. "Lecture? I wasn't going to lecture you. I was going to suggest it. Why do my children always think that I'm a prude?" She turned to Sharon McBride as she asked the question.

Sharon paused from taking food out of the bags. "Because for most of their life you've acted like one?"

Hannah threw back her head and laughed. "I think you may be right. If they only knew."

Brody and Brock both made gagging noises. The laughter was contagious. Blay leaned down and whispered in her ear, "How are you doing?"

She turned in his arms. "I'm doing pretty well. Your family is fantastic."

"They can be a bit too much. If you need me to send them packing, just let me know." Blay leaned down for a kiss. A loud, "Awww," from all the women seated around the coffee table started both her and Blay laughing. He shook his head. "Did I mention they can be a bit too much at times?"

Dawn leaned back in her office chair and groaned. It had been three weeks since her house had burned down. She'd taken three days off and then returned to work. Trying to find a new normal had been difficult. She'd grown accustomed to living alone, even though Blay had started to spend a lot of time at her house. Living together had its challenges. It wasn't like playing house. Blay had his schedule, and she had hers. Every so often, the two schedules would collide. It wasn't anything drastic. They learned to adapt, which was probably what all new couples did.

Clyde strolled out of his office and dropped a stack of documentation in her inbox. "These can wait until tomorrow. Don't stay all night."

"I have a couple of hours' more work. Remember, tomorrow I'm taking the afternoon off, and the entire day Friday." She was meeting with an architect that Killian recommended to draw up the plans for her new house. She had the money in savings to pay for the blueprints. However, because the fire had been declared arson, the insurance company wouldn't be paying out until the police finished their report and declared her innocent. Even though Sean had told the insurance company she was not a person of interest, they were adamant that they would not pay out until the case was closed.

"Oh, that's right, the big wedding." Clyde crossed his arms over his chest. "It looks like the weather will cooperate."

"Hannah King wouldn't have it any other way." Dawn chuckled because it was true. The woman had been a whirlwind of coordination, management, and delegation. Ryker and Brie were going to have a gorgeous wedding in the backyard of the King and McBride family homes.

"How's the new HR specialist? I haven't heard any complaints." Clyde sat on her desk as he spoke.

"She's only been here a week. I'm giving her time to settle in before I send her all of our problem children." She'd interviewed ten new applicants the week she returned from her little arson vacation. Eventually, she settled on a highly qualified candidate, although why the woman settled for HRNC logistics with her resumé was a question. Her references had been almost impossible to track down. Dawn eventually emailed them to make contact and all of them gave glowing recommendations

"As long as she takes some of the weight off your shoulders, I'll be happy. The sooner we can move you into a management position on the operations side of the house, the better. I've been talking to Paul, who has repeatedly told me I'm stupid for not utilizing you to your full potential. Don't tell him I told you so, but I believe he is correct. Speaking of my husband, he wants me to reschedule our dinner. When will you and Blay be available?"

"I'll ask him tomorrow. He's off and going with me to the architect's. You know, you and Paul could come over to the apartment and have dinner with us." She loved going out to eat, but since the house fire, she hadn't been in the mood to celebrate.

"That's fine. Let me know the date and time, and we'll be there. I know you've been avoiding rescheduling, and I can make guesses as to why. I haven't told Paul, but he's figuring it out. If you don't want him smack dab in your business, come out to dinner." Clyde knocked on her desk as he stood. "I'm going home. You should too."

"Guilty. What can I say? I haven't been in a celebratory mood lately. But I will ask Blay tomorrow, and we will reschedule. I promise."

"Good, you need some time away from the office. Don't think I don't see how many hours you work." Clyde ambled to the door. "And don't think I didn't notice you ignored my request that you go home. I know Blay's working, so there is nobody at the apartment."

"Thor and Oden are with Gage until he goes to bed at eight. I'll be home by then." She pointed to the stack of documents he just dropped on her desk. "I'll take a look at these, prioritize them, and then head out." She turned and watched as Clyde stared at her from the office door.

"Not a minute later." He pointed a finger at her.

"It's a promise." She watched him walk out the

door and then turned back to the work on her desk. Not that she wanted to go through it right now. The only thing she wanted to do was curl up on the couch at Blay's apartment. It wasn't depression. Escapism, perhaps. But she was doing more every day. Sean had cleared three of the five people she had fired. The other two couldn't be found, which was surprising, but they didn't have any families listed on their employment records. So, perhaps they had drifted. Ellen had been behaving herself, although Sean hadn't been able to locate her to speak to her. That little bit of information niggled at Dawn like an acid-tipped spear. If she hadn't done anything wrong, why wouldn't she talk to the police? That thought went around and around in her head like a merry-go-round on speed. Perhaps she was fixating on Ellen, although she really didn't know why. Ellen hadn't called Blay again. The texts and emails were relatively benign, considering the past emails and texts she had sent. Maybe the one-sided conversation Dawn had with her had actually worked. But, for some reason, she doubted it. More likely, the woman was mounting an attack from another direction.

Whatever. Dawn attacked the paperwork.

A knock at the executive office door got her

attention. She glanced up and smiled at her new HR specialist. "Peggy, what are you still doing here?"

"Just checking in before I head home for the night. Can we set up a time tomorrow or Friday after work so we can discuss details and go over some of the cases that you have yet to send me?" The friendly smile on Peggy's face alleviated some of the truth to the statement.

"I'm sorry about that. I guess I'm kind of a control freak." She laughed, and Peggy laughed with her. "I'm leaving early tomorrow, and I have an event on Friday, so how about we do it next Monday? Clyde leaves about six or six-thirty, so meet me here about six forty-five?"

"Or we could do it now?" Peggy took a step into the office just as Dawn's phone rang. She picked it up and looked at the face. She laughed a bit as she swiped the phone to answer the call. "It's not 8 o'clock yet, Clyde."

"I'm just checking to make sure that you're not staying." Clyde chuckled from the other end of the connection.

"No, I was just getting ready to leave, and Peggy stopped in to visit." She threw a smile in Peggy's direction.

"Peggy? Do you mean the new HR specialist?

Why is she still there? She does realize she's on salary, right?" Clyde hit her with the rapid-fire questions.

"Don't worry. We are walking out of the office as soon as I hang up." She rolled her eyes at her boss.

"See that you do, or I'll send an escort to make sure you both leave. As a matter of fact, that sounds like a wonderful idea. Have a good night!" Dawn looked at the phone and then laughed. "Clyde is sending an escort to make sure that we leave for the evening. He's a little bit overprotective."

Peggy glanced behind her and then into the executive office. "An escort? Who would be an escort?"

Dawn switched off her computer and picked up her purse. "During the week, there are offices open later. I'm sure he's probably calling IT and asking one of the guys to come up and make sure we're gone. Pro-tip: if you want to work uninterrupted, come in on the weekend. I normally spend a couple of hours on Saturday or Sunday when my boyfriend is working." She moved to the door where Peggy was waiting. They walked out, and Dawn shut and locked the executive offices. "Come on. I'll walk you out."

Peggy fell into step beside her. "How long have you worked here?"

"I started as a temp-hire when I was in college. After college, Clyde took me on full-time. I worked up from that temporary position to office manager, and that encompassed just about everything from HR to timekeeping to physical property management. Only recently has Clyde agreed to allow me to divest myself of some of those responsibilities. Hence you being here."

"That must take a lot of time away from you and your boyfriend." Peggy waited for Dawn to slide her card through the checkout point and exit the door.

Dawn waited for Peggy to repeat the process to check herself out of the building before she answered, "Not really. My boyfriend is a firefighter. He works twenty-four hours on, forty-eight hours off. So, anytime I do spend over and above is when he's working a full shift."

"A firefighter? Aren't you the lucky one?" Peggy chuckled. "How long have you been dating?"

"It's been almost six months now." She smiled as they walked down the steps. In the five and a half months since she said yes to Blay's repeated request to go out, her life had changed, mainly for good—arsonists aside. "This is me." Dawn pointed to her newly painted car.

"And I'm over there." Peggy pointed to a flashy

sports car. "Maybe I'll catch you this weekend if you are working. If not, I'll see you Monday night."

"I won't be working Saturday. If I work at all, it will be Sunday. And don't tell Clyde I told you how quiet the weekends were." She opened the door to her car as Peggy walked to hers.

"You can trust me. I'll never tell." Peggy waved and sank into her car.

CHAPTER 13

B lay sat with Dawn and watched his sister marry Ryker Terrell. The yard looked spectacular, and Brie was so damn happy it radiated off her like a beacon. The arbor they'd created had yellow and white roses weaved through the lattice. Bekki and Caitlyn had worked on it all morning. Each rosebud was in a small water vase attached to the flower stem which allowed them to stay fresh all day.

His sister wore a knee-length white lace dress with a shoulder-length veil. His sisters and the McBride girls wore different shades of yellow and carried smaller versions of the yellow and white rose bouquet that Brie held now. There wasn't a cloud in the sky.

He glanced at his mom, who was quietly dabbing her eyes. She'd worked so hard to give Brie a wedding she'd love. As much as they all gave her a rough time about being a Hover Mother, the woman would bleed for each of them.

Dawn leaned over to him as the soloist from his mom's church sang. "The vows were beautiful."

He smiled down at her. He'd thought so, too. He'd imagined himself and Dawn up there in front of their friends and family. He wasn't given to flights of fancy, but he had no doubt that was where they were heading, too. When the singer finished, the minister had Brie and Ryker turn toward the crowd. "Ladies and gentlemen, what God has joined together, let no man put asunder. May I present Mr. and Mrs. Ryker Terrell. Ryker, you may kiss your bride."

And kiss her he did. Ryker grabbed Brie and dipped her until she shrieked and grabbed hold of him. He kissed her long and hard. Laughter bubbled through the small crowd. When he righted his bride, they walked down the aisle to the porch which had been decorated and held a banquet of epic proportions. His mom and Sharon had worked tirelessly to make the feast. Dawn and he had come over early this morning to help with the last-minute details, which he was happy to do.

KRIS MICHAELS

They waited until his mom and dad and Colm
and Sharon were escorted down the aisle. Ryker's
mom had passed, so he'd asked the McBrides to sit
with his brothers on his side of the aisle.

Dawn held onto his arm. The grass and high
heels weren't exactly a match made in heaven. As
soon as they approached the porch, Dawn kicked off
the strappy sandals and threw them in a pile of high-
heeled women's shoes. Blay glanced around. Every
female in the wedding party was barefoot. "Thank
God." Dawn wiggled her toes and sighed happily.

They made their way through the reception line,
and he hugged and slapped Ryker on the back. The
guy was solid, both in construction and emotionally.
Ryker loved his sister, and that made him perfect. He
kissed Brie and told her that he loved her. She was
the sister that had always mothered him. He and
Bekki were too close in age to do anything but
bicker and fight when they were young. Brie settled
their arguments and listened when he had issues he
didn't want to take to his mom or dad. He was damn
happy she'd found Ryker.

They drank champagne and toasted the bride
and groom before everyone went through the buffet
line. After they were all seated, Xander, Ryker's
brother and best man, tapped on his glass. "Ladies

and gentlemen, may I have your attention, please." Blay turned in his chair so that he could see the bridal table. "Thank you. As the best man, I believe it falls to me to make a speech. As a lawyer, speaking won't be a problem, although Ryker has warned me to be brief. He's bossy like that."

Xander waited until the laughter faded before he turned to Ryker. "There was never a moment that I questioned my brother's love for me or the brat pack over there." He motioned toward their other brothers. "Life wasn't always easy for Ryker. He worked hard for everything he accomplished, and he had a drawer full of commendations and citations when he retired. Now, he's working with us as our project manager, and let me tell you, when Ryker speaks, everyone listens. Again, that bossy trait shines through. His best accomplishment, however, is finding and keeping Brie. She is the reason that relationships have been mended, truths have been revealed, and our family has healed. For that, we will be eternally grateful. To Brie and Ryker, two of the best people I know. May you have love, health, happiness, and prosperity for the rest of your lives."

Blay lifted his glass with everyone else, toasting the couple. Tara's speech lasted a bit longer as she told funny childhood stories but ended on an emotional note. "Brie, you are my best friend, a sister of choosing if not by blood, and nobody but Ryker could ever be the man that you deserve. May God bless both of you."

Dawn leaned into him after they finished the champagne. They watched the first dance and then the dance with the parents. Ryker danced with Blay's mother and then Sharon. Brie danced with their dad. He could see how emotional it was for his old man.

After that, the beer coolers appeared, and a multitude of wine bottles were uncorked. Blay lost his tie and jacket. They danced and laughed until well after the bride and groom slipped away. When it was only family left, which included the McBrides, they pulled out the lawn chairs and visited until family started drifting away, too.

Dawn sat on his lap, her head on his shoulder. "It was a lovely day." She sighed the words.

"It was nice." He agreed and rubbed her back. "Are you ready to go home?"

She nodded and yawned. "But I need to check with your mom to see if she needs help."

"You don't need to do that." Amber and Brody strolled back from the house. "Everything that needs refrigeration has been moved. Hannah and Sharon said they have everything else covered. Gage is spending the night here, and I'll come by to pick him up in the morning. If she needs any help, I'll call in reinforcements."

Brody nodded to the street. "Do you need someone to drive you home?"

Blay snorted. *Typical big brother.* "No, I stopped drinking hours ago."

Brody yawned. "All right then. See you tomorrow."

Dawn got up as Brody and Amber walked to the street. "Come on. Let's go say goodnight to your folks and then head home."

He stood up and tugged her into him. "Home. That sounds nice." He dropped a kiss on her lips. "I like living with you."

"Even when I leave the top off the toothpaste?" She smiled up at him.

"It's something I'll have to learn to live with." He just screwed the top on, although he teased her about it. "Just like you'll have to learn to live with my socks never finding the laundry hamper."

Dawn tried to hide a smile. "That's a tough one to overcome."

"I've tried teaching Oden and Thor to put them in the laundry." He had, and the attempt was hilarious and a complete failure.

"I can't blame them, poor babies. Who would want to put a dirty sock in their mouth?" Dawn teased him as they broke apart and headed into the house. "It was cool that Killian took them and Duke to the construction site today. They'll love running all day with Duke."

"Yeah, Killian's foreman is a dog guy, and he's staying at the site tonight so Killian can have the night off. So, we will probably have very spoiled and antsy dogs tomorrow."

"Ah, well, we can run the energy out of them." He squeezed her hand, acknowledging her comment. She hadn't wanted to go running lately, so even the mention of them running together was good in his opinion. For a while, that damn fire seemed to beat her down, but she was a fighter. He had no doubt she'd bounce back.

They found his parents and said good night before Dawn collected her heels, and they walked out to his truck. He helped her in and then fired up the truck to head home.

About three miles from the apartment, his phone rang. Brody's name. "Ten bucks he wants me to stop for takeout."

Dawn yawned. "I'm too tired to eat."

He swiped the face, and the truck picked up the call. "Hello."

"Blay, did you leave your door unlocked today?" Brody's voice was deadly serious.

"No." He glanced at Dawn, who was now wide awake. "I locked it. Dawn was with me when I did."

"Where are you?"

"About five minutes away."

"Stay outside. Amber and I are going to clear your apartment. Shit, I can see pry marks." The line went dead.

"Someone broke into your apartment. How? They'd have to get into the lobby first." Dawn asked the same question he was thinking.

"I don't know." He stepped on the gas and pulled into his parking slot just before a patrol car pulled up in front of the apartment building.

Amber came out of the lobby. "Blay, go on up. Dawn, stay here with me."

Blay sprinted up the stairs and through the main doors. Glass was scattered on the floor. A large chunk was missing by the lock. He jogged up the stairs and stepped into his apartment. Red paint sprayed across the walls. 'Fucking Bitch, he's mine', and other words he wouldn't ever say in front of his mother were emblazoned in two-feet-tall letters. He stood there and looked at the damage. His couch had been knifed open. The white nylon stuffing was strewn across the room. He moved forward and looked into the kitchen. Food had been slung from the refrigerator onto the floor, but there was no other damage.

"In here. Don't touch anything." Brody's appearance at the hall to his bathroom jolted him into action. He moved across the trashed living room and followed his brother. All of Dawn's new clothes were strewn across the room. Everything had been cut or torn, and everything reeked of gasoline.

"Ellen."

Brody nodded. "There is no other suspect here, Blay. I've called Sean. He'll want to see this, too. But she didn't start the fire. The question is why?" Brody carefully backed out of the room, and Blay followed suit. "Why hasn't Sean been able to find her?" Brody motioned the path Blay needed to walk. "We'll get the crime scene techs here shortly."

"I have no idea where she is staying. She hasn't asked for an in-person meeting since I went upstate to her apartment."

Brody nodded and crossed his arms, staring at the mess. "Once the detectives get here, they'll want to know, including her address upstate. Has she made any threats against you?"

"Threats? She went to my job and tried to get me fired. She showed up at home and upset Mom. The one constant theme in her emails and texts was that I would be sorry. Has she outright said she was going to hurt me? No. Look at this. It's not me she's mad at. I think it's Dawn she is fixated on."

"The two of you can stay upstairs with us. It's going to take several coats of paint to cover up the shit, plus we need to blot up that gasoline and get rid of the furniture that is soaked in it." Brody waved to the words on the wall and then back toward the bedroom.

"I don't want Dawn to see this."

"Too late." Dawn stepped into the apartment. "Why?" She stepped further into the room and swung her attention to the other wall. Blay watched her pale as she read the words. "What have I ever done to this woman?"

"You can't make sense of the actions of an irrational person. So, why don't we all step out and let the detectives process the scene." Amber stepped in behind Dawn. Two detectives in suits followed her in the door. "This is Detective Hodgins and Detective Meriwether, Robbery, HCPD." Amber made the introductions.

Detective Meriwether shook Blay's and Brody's hands. "We met Dawn downstairs. I understand that Blay is the owner of the apartment?"

Blay nodded his head. "I am."

"All right. We're going to need a statement from you and also from Dawn. We'll also need to interview the occupants of the building to see if they noticed anything else amiss." Meriwether pulled out a small tablet.

"I own the third-floor apartment," Brody informed the detective. "We were at the same event with Blay and Dawn. Our sister's wedding."

God, he wished he hadn't taken the dogs to Killian's work site, although leaving them cooped up all day wasn't an option either. But still, Thor would have stopped her. Odin may have licked her to death, but...

Hodgins put on a pair of blue latex gloves. "Do you have any idea as to who may have done this?"

Blay put his arm around Dawn as he spoke, "I believe it would be a woman from my past. She claims that I'm the father of her baby, yet she won't prove it with a DNA test. I've received harassing phone calls from her, I have a restraining order against her, and I have all the documentation and copies of emails and the texts that I can provide."

Meriwether nodded her head. "It sounds like you've done all the right things. However, it would appear that her harassment has escalated."

Brody cleared his throat and sent Blay a look. "There is a possibility that this woman also set fire to Dawn's home about three weeks ago."

"What?" Dawn jumped as if she'd been hit.

"You can't deny the possibility, babe." Blay tried to comfort her.

"What is the name of this woman?" Meriwether stood with pen and paper in hand.

"Ellen Margaret Smith." Blay freely gave the information that he had to the detectives. Dawn stood with him throughout the entire process, her eyes locked on the words on the wall. When the detectives and the crime scene technicians were done, Blay resecured the door to the best of his ability, then they followed Amber and Brody upstairs.

Amber gave Dawn some pajamas and something to wear in the morning. Amber had to go to work early but wanted to make sure her sister was taken care of. Once they settled into bed in Brody's spare room, he pulled her into him.

"I'm so sorry, babe."

"She's dangerous." Dawn shivered and moved closer to him.

"She is. I want you to be extra careful going to and from work." If there were a way he could avoid work and still pay his bills, he'd shadow Dawn until they caught Ellen.

"I can't let her destroy my life, Blay." Dawn elbowed up and looked down at him. "I'll be careful, but I won't be a victim any longer. Right now, I'm mad. I'm so damn mad. What right does she have to destroy my life? When the police find her, I want answers." Dawn flopped back. "The bitch."

Blay rolled over on his side to look at her. "Until she is brought in, make sure that you let somebody know where you're going and what you're doing. I know it will be a pain in the ass, but we don't know how far she'll go. Right now, it's only property damage. There is no telling what she'll do next."

Dawn flipped onto her side and stared back at him. "I almost wish that she'd come after me. If she weren't pregnant, I'd go after her. I haven't had a girl fight since I was in the eighth grade, but I'm telling you, I could pull some serious hair, but my nails were always cut short, so scratching was out."

Blay chuckled and wrapped his arm around her

waist, pulling her closer. "I bet you were a little hellcat even without the nails, weren't you?"

Dawn sighed. "No, not really. But Debbie Masterson was mean to me the entire year, and I had enough. So, I pushed her down and pulled her hair. I got a great big clump of it, too." Dawn laughed softly. "She came to school the next day with a short haircut. I felt victorious. And then I felt horrible. I'm not a mean person, but I can be pushed too far."

"You're the best person I know. I love you, Dawn. I'm sorry my past has crashed into our present."

She reached up and cupped his face with her hand. "Don't be. You were completely honest. I could've bailed at any time. But I don't want to. You've become incredibly important to me, Blayze Benedict King. I watched that ceremony today. I could picture us up there someday."

Blay smiled at her. "Did you just ask me to marry you?"

Dawn's eyes popped open. "Ah, maybe?" She pushed Blay onto his back and lifted over his chest. "Would that scare you, big man?"

"Not in the slightest." Blay lifted a bit and took her lips with his. When the kiss ended, he whispered against her lips, "Yes, I'll marry you."

Dawn laughed as she dropped for a kiss. "Do I

need to buy you a ring now?" Blay ran his fingers down her ribs, tickling her. She squealed and giggled as she rolled off him. "Stop, we'll wake up Amber and Brody."

"There's no way they are asleep already." Blay stretched over her.

"That doesn't make the situation any better. It's kind of creepy that my sister can hear me with my boyfriend."

"Fiancé." Blay trailed kisses down her neck as he reminded her, "You asked, I accepted."

Her fingers trailed up his back, and she whispered, "It was a joke. We haven't known each other long enough to make that kind of commitment."

Blay continued his trail of kisses over her collarbone. "How long does it take to fall in love?"

"Love isn't the only factor in making a relationship work." Her hands slid to the base of his neck and through his hair. She gripped tightly when his tongue found the hardened nipple of her breast.

"Love is the *only* factor that matters in a relationship." He dipped down again and teased the other nipple for a moment. He lifted so he could see her in the pale light coming through the bedroom window. "Nothing else exists without it. Love makes everything possible. Do you love me?"

"So much so that it scares me." Her voice shook with the honesty of her words.

"Never be afraid of me. Never question my love. I'm not a monk, as you well know. I've looked for love. I've looked for what we have now. I never found it until you. You are the reason I feel the way I do. I've witnessed love that has transcended death. That depth of emotion is what I feel for you." Blay stared at her as he spoke.

"I feel it too. I'm just afraid that it's going too fast. I guess I'm also afraid that one day you'll wake up and realize I'm not the prize you seem to think I am." She shook her head. "I'm afraid of being alone again."

"I'll never leave you. I'll spend my life proving that to you." Blay dropped for a kiss. He would prove to her that he was hers forever. He took his time making love to her. There was no sense of urgency, only of contact. He needed to know she was with him, and he felt that right now she needed that, too.

Slowly, he took the time to rediscover her body. They'd made love before, but tonight, he wanted to show her just how much she meant to him.

His lips, fingers, and tongue tasted every inch of her body. Her soft moans urged him forward. As he centered over her and entered her hot core, he dropped for a kiss. "I'll spend my life proving my love to you."

He rode the crest of her release and let his orgasm wash over him before he realized he didn't have a condom on. He jolted and then settled immediately. After a lifetime of being extra careful, it was a knee-jerk reaction, but her birth control was in full effect.

Dawn shook her head and chuckled. It didn't take a genius to figure out why he'd jumped. "We're good. I have us covered." Yeah, he guessed it didn't take a rocket scientist to figure out what he'd freaked about.

Blay dropped his head to her shoulder. "Dear God, I almost had a heart attack."

Dawn's low, throaty laugh as she stroked his back sent a shiver down his spine. "It wouldn't be impossible to manage two babies in diapers."

"Two?" Blay's brain wasn't computing. Blood had pooled elsewhere, which wasn't helping his brain function.

"Well, if Ellen's child is yours, there's no way we'll let her raise that baby. Especially now that we believe she's a criminal." Dawn shook her head. "I have some savings, and I can help with lawyer bills, or if we're going to live in your apartment, we can use some of the money from the insurance settlement to pay for a lawyer."

Blay stared down at her. "You're serious?" That Dawn would take on another child, one that wasn't hers, and be willing to pay the legal fees was nothing less than amazing.

"Dead serious. That child deserves a shot at a decent life. If she's yours, she's mine." Dawn stroked his cheek with her fingertips.

A smile spread across his face. "She? That's the second time you said you wanted a girl."

Dawn rolled her eyes. "Again, you fixated on that. Not the part where I said if she's part of you, she's part of us."

"Oh, I got that. I heard what you said. It's kind of amazing how you can tell me how much you love me without saying the words." Blay dropped for another kiss.

"Sometimes actions speak louder than words. Come here, big boy, let me show you again."

CHAPTER 14

Blay dropped down from the fire truck and connected the exhaust hose as the truck backed into the fire station. They'd worked their asses off this shift. Three automobile accidents, a premature birth, and one kitchen fire, all before lunch. Well, what was supposed to be lunch. He glanced at the digital clock on the wall. It was almost three. Royal was cooking today, so the man handed his turnout gear over to Blay, and he made sure that it was set up for deployment should they get called out again. He also took over Royal's chores so the man could get food on the table. They were all hungry, and Blay was in a particular mood. The cops hadn't been able to find Ellen, and the address he'd given them upstate had turned out to be a short-term rental. The name on the rental the date he'd gone up there was a sixty-year-old man who had no idea what the cops were talking about when they tracked him down.

To complicate matters further, Ellen Margaret Smith didn't exist. At least, not in Hope City or the state of Baltimore.

So, everything Ellen had told him was a lie. Which, in reality, should surprise him, but it didn't. His gut told him he wasn't the father of her baby. She'd dropped off the face of the earth.

The only time his phone vibrated was when Dawn texted him with her plans. Until they knew for sure that Ellen was out of their lives, he wasn't going to let Dawn take any chances.

They'd spent the last two weeks in a state of hyper-vigilance. He took a day off without telling her, and he and Rory painted and cleaned the apartment. It took five coats of paint to cover the spray paint, but he'd have put ten coats on it to get it back the way it was.

He and Dawn picked out the replacement couch together and settled on a sectional with a chaise on one end and a recliner, leather again. They both stretched out on the chaise when they watched Bekki on the news. Then, of course, they'd christened the new furniture in an array of different positions. That had been fun. The bed they'd bought was christened in the same way—with enthusiasm.

Blay made his way into the kitchen after finishing his chores. "Call everyone, would you?" Royal asked as he pulled his famous biscuits out of the oven. Blay didn't need to be asked twice. He gathered the crew, and they sat down at the table. The massive pot of chili that Royal had whipped up was destroyed in no time. The biscuits, slathered in butter, were heaven. After lunch, everyone pitched in to clean up. Since it was Sunday, the crew migrated to the television and bickered over what movie to watch. Blay laughed at the antics of grown men. Hopefully, the afternoon would pass without—

The klaxon went off again. The crew rose as one and headed to the truck. The medical team alert sounded next, followed by a call out of three other stations. Whatever was happening was big. Blay dropped his turnout gear, toed off his tennis shoes, and stepped into his boots, pulling his suspenders up. He grabbed the handle and hefted himself up to the seat he was assigned. He and Royal looked at each other when the Captain hit them up with the details. "Apartment fire. Seventh floor of a fifteen-story building. Fire and smoke are visible on the seventh floor. Fire suppression system is not working."

Blay closed his eyes and mentally ran through the procedures for clearing the upper floors. "Access from the roof?" he asked as he opened his eyes.

"Unknown," the Lieutenant's reply came back to him over the headset.

He swore to himself.

Royal cocked his head and mouthed, *You okay?*

He gave his partner a thumbs up and mouthed, *Good to go*.

They were number three engine on scene, so he and Royal packed on the rest of their safety gear, and when they were ready, the Captain informed the Battalion Commander they were available.

Blay glanced up at the old brownstone. It was a code nightmare. However, there was an outside fire escape that snaked up the building. Two sets of entry teams were scaling the building, and Blay and Royal joined the climb at the BC's instruction. They were assigned to clear the upper floors, starting at the top and working down. When the entry team on seventh finished, they would start on the eighth because they would know where the hot spots were and where to be cautious. Going through the floor was always a risk.

He heard a fourth team dispatched as he and Royal cleared the fifteenth floor. They worked through the fourteenth and thirteenth. Dark smoke rolled through the apartments on the twelfth floor. "BC, this is Entry Team Three. We have heavy smoke on thirteen, heat from the floor." There was smoke snaking up from the cracks in the floorboards. Royal called it in. They'd made the call as to who would handle the comms at the beginning of each shift.

"Roger. We have entry teams on ten. Standby Team Three," the BC acknowledged their concern and then radioed the other teams.

"Affirm. Heat from above," the other team acknowledged, and the BC dispatched the ladder company to find the source of the fire.

Blay and Royal carefully advanced, Blay carrying the W-tool. When they reached the first apartment door, Royal tried the handle and announced them. He waited ten seconds before he stood aside. Blay slung the twenty-five-pound multipurpose tool from his back to a position he could use as a battering ram and took a step back.

His foot hit nothing but air, and he went down.

As he fell, he flailed his arms, trying to find a grip to stop his fall. The hallway one floor down did that. The damn tool, still on its sling, crashed down on his hand, pinning it to the floor. He heard Royal's voice from a distance. The searing pain in his hand and arm mandated he roll to try to get the heavy weight off his hand.

As he rolled, another chunk of ceiling fell. He braced for the impact, tucking his head and shielding as much of his body as he could. The weight of the debris knocked his breath away. The heat up against him was intolerable. He fought to move, screamed Royal's name, and pawed at the damn W-tool that still had his hand pinned to the floor. His oxygen alarm sounded somewhere in the distance. Blay fought against the darkness that swamped the corners of his vision. He fought against the pain of the fire, the weight of the debris, and the thought that he'd never see Dawn again.

The searing hot material moved, and he scrambled to get out from under the heat, but his body wouldn't listen to his mind.

Hands reached him and pulled.

"Pinned! My hand!" He screamed the words.

The pulling stopped, and Royal crawled under the searing hot chunk of debris. "Don't drop that bitch, guys. I don't want to be roasted alive," Royal growled as he reached Blay's hand. "Fuck dude, you're not pinned. You're skewered. Hold on. This is going to hurt like a bitch."

Royal picked up the W-tool and struck down. The first blow forced a scream from him. The second… Well, he'd never remember it.

The darkness overtook him.

Damn, what a fucking headache. He shifted and groaned. *What the hell?* He blinked his eyes open and stared up at fluorescent lights. *Not where I should be.* He rolled his head and brought the white curtains into focus. His Lieutenant and his Captain were there, talking to each other. *Why? About what? Think, damn it.* He closed his eyes for a moment. The fire. His hand began to throb in a weird, distant way. He opened his eyes again and turned his head to the right. A piece of jagged metal stuck out of the back of his hand and was embedded in a small piece of wood cupped in his palm.

"Fuck."

As if his words started the world, a scurry of people appeared. Royal's face was over his. "You're going into surgery. They have a surgeon specializing in hand injuries doing the gig in the operating room. It isn't as bad as it looks. You'll be fine."

"Dawn. Call Dawn."

"I called your brother. He said he'd make all the calls."

A nurse told Royal to get out of the way, and then the fluorescent lights started to fly past rapidly. He lifted his head. No, the lights weren't moving. He was. He was being wheeled out of the curtained-off area.

He was conscious until the anesthesiologist came by to ask him if he was allergic to anything and if he'd ever been under before. He answered and then counted backward from ten. He made it to eight.

He woke up with some fuzzy memories of waking up after the surgery, but the room he was in was different than it was before. He turned his head to look at his hand. His arm was supported, and a hard plastic mold under his hand was cushioned with about an inch of soft cotton between the skin and the mold. An elastic bandage wrapped the entire thing into something resembling a club. He stared at his fingers and made each one move just a bit. He shifted and winced. His back was sore, but he knew the cause of that: the heat of the debris and weight of the ceiling as it hit him, no doubt. Since he was laying on his back, it wasn't a second or third-degree burn, just damn sore from the blow when the roof came down on him. He wiggled his toes and moved his feet. His other hand had an IV running into the vein on the back. He could move the arm and his fingers.

The door to his room opened. His father walked in along with his Battalion Commander. "How bad is it?" He wanted the truth, and he knew his dad would give it to him.

"They aren't sure. The surgeon said the repair went well. Time will tell." His dad didn't pull any punches.

His BC waited until Blay looked at him. "Of course, you'll be on medical leave until you're able to return. Then you'll be assigned to your new position as an engineer. Congratulations, son. I just found out about an hour ago."

Blay gave his BC a weak smile. "Depending on the rehab of my hand, of course."

The man nodded. "I know what stock you come from. You'll be back on a crew before you know it."

Blay glanced down at the bandaged club. "Might be a week or two."

The BC chuckled. "I'll give you three just for good measure. You take care, son."

"Sir?" Blay called out to the officer.

The BC turned around and cocked his head.

"Did everyone get out?"

The man drew a deep breath and put his hands in his pockets. "No. This was a coordinated suicide—one victim on the seventh floor, one on the eleventh. The fire on the seventh was so much bigger that no one noticed the fire on the eleventh until the crews arrived. The person who committed suicide on the eleventh used a slow accelerant but left the bottle beside them in the bedroom. We were able to deduce from the audiotapes it exploded just as you stepped back to use the W-tool. Perfect timing."

"Or not so perfect." His dad shrugged.

"Right. I'll let you talk. If you need anything, King, let me know." The BC walked out the door.

"Your mom was sitting with you, but the nurses asked her to step out until the doctor made his rounds before going home tonight."

Blay lifted an eyebrow. "I bet that floated as well as a lead zeppelin."

"Not even that well. Dawn is here now. Traffic

getting across town was insane. She'll come in as soon as the doctor clears out."

"How did you score special privileges?"

His dad opened his suit jacket and flashed his badge and gun. "I have a magic ticket into any location in this city."

Blay chuckled and rolled his head toward his hand. "What is the prognosis?"

"Again, they didn't say. The doctor that operated on you was here for an interview. The hospital doesn't have a hand specialist. Doctor Kendell had privileges here from a surgery he flew in to do at the beginning of the year. So, again, fortuitous timing."

Blay sighed. "I know it could have been worse. Is it wrong that I'm pissed that it happened at all?"

"No, son. You can get angry, just don't take it out on the ones you love." His dad leaned back against the wall. "I learned that lesson the hard way. You don't need to repeat it. Just trust me on it and find another way to channel your anger."

Blay snorted. "Between Ellen and this, I'm about ready to punch a hole through the wall."

"Not with that hand." His father lifted his chin and motioned toward his club.

"Right? Has there been any luck finding her?"

His father's lips tightened into a tight line. "No.

The name she gave you doesn't exist. We've run down the doctor records at the OB/GYN she went to upstate. Based on the date, one patient is no longer being seen by the doctor."

"Ellen."

"No, someone by the name of Margaret Paillon."

"Does she exist?"

"She does. She's eighty years old and a resident of the St. Francis nursing home in Kennebunkport, Maine. No children or nieces."

Blay shook his head slowly. "How can that be? Is she a freaking ghost?"

"I think she is a con woman who got caught up in her own game." His father shoved his hands in his pocket and braced one foot on the wall.

"But she hasn't tried to blackmail me."

His father's eyes lifted to his. "I don't have any facts to back up my theory, but I believe the entire scam revolved around you believing you were the father of her baby. Asking for a DNA test threw her. Then you refused to be baited into her crazy. Top that off with Dawn telling her she wasn't going anywhere... well, it would kick someone who wasn't too far away from sinking to spiral."

"Dad, I need this to end."

"It will, son, but not on your timetable."

"Do you think she's still out there? I haven't received a call or text in weeks."

His father's lips thinned again. "I would like to think she realized she wasn't going to get what she wanted, but I've talked to the forensic psychologists retained by the force. They caution against dismissing her. Arson, breaking and entering, defacing your apartment are all crimes, but they are concerned about the words on the walls and the way Dawn's clothes were destroyed. I don't think she's gone but rather waiting for an opportunity."

"I need you to talk to Dawn. She needs to understand the seriousness involved here."

His father lifted away from the wall and nodded. "I'll go do that now. When the doctors clear you for visitors, I'll send her back." His dad gripped his foot under the bed and squeezed it. "And don't scare the hell out of your mom and me again, okay?"

Blay smiled. "Sorry, I wasn't planning on falling through the floor today."

"That's good to know. Get some rest." His dad winked at him and walked out the door.

CHAPTER 15

Dawn followed the nurse down the long hallway. Her hands were shaking, but not because she was worried about Blay. His father had assured her that he would be okay and that he was awake and doing well. What he'd said next, though, had rocked her world. She rubbed her arms as she walked slightly behind the nurse. Chauncey had cautioned her in no uncertain terms that Ellen, if that was really her name, was dangerous. She mentally rolled her eyes. As if the arson and breaking and entering weren't bad enough, the forensic psychologists said the mutilation of her clothes was personal and a direct threat. Her facade of having her life together shattered in front of Hannah and Chauncey. She'd lost it. The relief of

Blay being okay and the threat of Ellen intensifying crashed into a maelstrom of emotions. Hannah held her and stroked her hair. Amber sat on the other side of her in the waiting room, her hand on Dawn's leg as Hannah comforted her.

She wiped at her cheeks to ensure they weren't damp before she followed the nurse to Blay's door. "He may be asleep. You can stay as long as you want."

She opened the door and stepped in.

Blay dwarfed the hospital bed. His hand was elevated on a wedge of foam and wrapped in what looked like cotton batting. He had several scrapes and cuts on his face, but he looked so damn good. She could tell he was asleep, so she quietly took a seat in the corner.

As she stared at Blay, her mother came to mind. She would have loved Blay. Her dad would have, too. Her parents had the best marriage, unlike her father's first marriage that produced Amber. His ex-wife was a shrew, and that woman messed up poor Amber in more ways than one. Dawn had been blessed with two parents that loved her uncondi-tionally. Her mom was her best friend. Maybe that's why she wanted to have a little girl someday. She wanted to have that connection with her daughter.

The sun slowly dipped over the horizon until the

room grew dark. Blay stirred and groaned. She was up and by his side in a second. "Hey, do you need something?"

He stilled and looked at her. "Only you."

She leaned down and kissed him. "Well, lucky you, I'm here. Nice hand you got there."

Blay gave a small chuckle. "Personally, I'm calling it a club."

She turned and looked at the wrap job. "I can see that. How are you feeling?"

"Sore, but it's not too bad. I took a step back and there was no floor."

"Royal said you fell to the next story."

"I did. I thought the W-tool had pinned my hand, but it was impaled on some metal."

"What did the doctor say?" She lowered the silver bar and sat down next to him, putting his hand with the IV onto her lap.

"He wants to write it up in a medical journal. The metal was so hot that it cauterized the cut as it went through. He had to repair six bones in the back of my hand but was confident that I'd have full use of my hand again with physical therapy. Did Dad talk to you about Ellen?"

She nodded. "He scared the crap out of me, yes."

He moved the fingers of his good hand, and she

placed her hand over his. "I don't want you to be scared. I want you to be prepared in case she does something stupid. Be aware of your environment."

"I have been, and I will continue to be. I promise. I told Clyde you'd had an accident, and he gave me the rest of this week and next week off. I'll pop in this weekend to take care of the important things that he needs done, but that will only take a couple of hours. The rest of the time, I'm going to be Nurse Dawn. Brody and Gage are taking care of the dogs. You've got nothing to worry about but getting rest so you can get out of here."

Blay's eyes darkened. "For a while there, I thought I wouldn't see you again."

Her eyes misted up again. "That can't happen. You promised me forever, remember?"

He smiled at her. "Forever." His eyes drifted shut again.

She leaned forward and kissed his forehead. "Forever and beyond." He'd told her of the couple in the car accident and how the man's last words had affected him. The way Blay explained the love he witnessed had touched her too. She wanted that kind of love with Blay.

Dawn watched out the window as Blay, Gage, Brody and the dogs crossed the street. After the dogs were in the park, Gage set his car down and then turned it on. The dogs jumped and barked, racing after the car. They followed, jumping in the air when the car turned so they wouldn't be touched by the big-wheeled radio-controlled car. They were in heaven. Brody had suggested the before-school playtime the night before, and both Gage and Blay were excited to experiment with the car and the dogs.

Her eyes drifted to Blay. This was his first foray out of the house in the three days since he'd come home from the hospital. She turned from the window and sped to the bedroom to change the sheets and open the windows. Her stubborn boyfriend-slash-kind-of-fiancé refused to take pain pills, and he was hurting. The dogs seemed to understand he was in pain and sprawled beside him on the couch or beside the bed, gentle giants protecting their human.

Dawn threw the sheets into the washer, grabbed fresh ones, made the bed, and then pulled out the vacuum and turned it on. Constant worry seemed to rest on her shoulders. Thoughts of Ellen were always lurking somewhere. The woman even crept into her dreams. Chauncey's warning had been dire.

He believed the woman wasn't finished, but the police couldn't find her.

She worked her way from the bedroom down the hall, vacuuming up small whisps of dog hair from the hardwood. Ellen had started with her texts and emails to Blay again. They reported each one. Detective Meriwether was fed all the information, but according to Chauncey, who checked in nightly with Blay, they were no closer to finding the woman.

Dawn unplugged the cord and moved it to an outlet in the living room. The whir of the vacuum buffered the outside world as she cleaned, letting her mind spin with questions that couldn't be answered. She moved a laptop Clyde had brought her from the couch to the coffee table. She was falling behind at work and hated that, but it couldn't be helped. Maybe she would drive over to the office on Saturday or Sunday to catch up and farm out her duties and responsibilities for the following week. Another stressor, but this one she could do something about.

She'd just finished vacuuming when Blay and the dogs came in the door. As Blay locked their new metal door to the new metal door frame, Oden trotted over to her for attention which she gladly gave. Thor went straight for his water bowl. Both of their tongues were hanging out, and they were panting.

"Success?" She tiptoed up and kissed Blay when he walked into the room.

"Absolutely. I need to get one of those things. They loved to chase it but never tried to catch it." Blay glanced at the vacuum. "You don't have to do that."

"Vacuum? Yes, I do. I have a miniature Oden in this canister."

"No, I mean I have one good hand. So, I can push that thing."

"You have two good hands. This is temporary, remember?" She wouldn't let him believe anything else. "Besides, you're still healing. When you're better, I'll lounge on the couch and watch you vacuum. Shirtless." She wiggled her eyebrows.

He chuckled and pulled her into a modified-side-ways-one-armed hug and rested his chin on the top of her head. "It's a deal. In the meantime, let's spend some time in the hot tub."

She lifted away from him and stared up at him. "The hot tub?" Blay was the only person she knew of that had a hot tub in his apartment. He'd installed it when he bought the place from Brody. It was a work of art, and hot tub sex with Blay was wonderful, sometimes wild, and always orgasmic. However, with his hand out of commission, they'd have to be a lot tamer.

He rubbed his hips against her, and she felt the imprint of his very interested cock against her belly. "Somebody is feeling better."

"I am. Help me wrap this, and I'll keep my arm propped along the back ledge."

"Ah, thought this through, have you?" She turned, keeping her arm around his waist, stepping forward, moving them toward the bathroom.

"It may have crossed my mind about a million times or so since I came home, yes."

"Only a million? I must be slipping. Wait here. I'll get the waterproofing kit." The nurse had explained the best way to wrap his hand to keep the moisture away. The waterproof tape secured the plastic just below his elbow. The only complication was Blay's arm now had a completely hairless strip where the tape pulled the hair on his arm off.

She finished waterproofing him and helped him get undressed and into the hot tub. Once he sat down and had his hand settled against the ledge, she turned on the jets and got undressed. "This always feels so decadent." She slid into the hot water and straddled Blay's legs.

"Yes, you do."

His uninjured hand found her waist. She bent down and kissed him. His interest laid hard between them. As hungry for him as he was for her, they didn't need or want a slow build-up. She reached between them and centered his shaft under her. Slowly, she lowered herself onto his cock. Hard and thick, Blay filled her. She lifted until just his head remained inside her and then lowered again, adding a slight swivel of her hips at the base. Blay's eyes closed, and his head fell back to the wall.

"Fuck, so good."

She braced her hands on his shoulders and continued the motion. It *was* good. *So damn good.* Her sighs mingled with his as she continued her movements. Chasing pleasure, she sped up and dropped a bit harder, needing the incredible friction to escalate. Her thighs burned, and she lost her rhythm.

Blay's hand on her hip stopped her. "Stay still."

She felt him move his legs and brace himself before he took over, bucking up from under her. She arched her back and grabbed his thighs, just above his knees. The change of position was cataclysmic and immediate. She orgasmed as Blay continued to push inside her, faster and deeper. Just as the rolls of sensation started to ebb, she fractured again. This time Blay came with her.

She stayed like she was, arched back, her hair half in the water. Blay's hand cupped her back and pulled her forward. Limp, she folded on top of him, her head on his shoulder. The warm water continued to bubble around them as she caught her breath.

"Are you okay?" She whispered the words as he stroked her back.

He chuckled, "Better than okay."

She pushed up so she could see him. "Your hand?"

"Fine." He kissed her softly. "Have I told you today how much I love you?"

She lifted an eyebrow. "Twice within the last few minutes."

He blinked. "Twice?"

She nodded and smiled. "Oh, yeah. You're a hot tub god."

"Do you think I should put that on my resumé?" He laughed as he spoke.

"Nope. You have a full-time position. No need for a resumé." She pushed his hair out of his eyes. "Are you happy?"

The smirk on his face faded. He stared at her. "Beyond happy. I love you, and I want to spend the rest of my life with you."

She smiled. "Did you just ask me to marry you?"

Blay stared at her. "No, but *this* is me asking you. Dawn Swanson, will you marry me?"

She reached forward and put both of her hands on his shoulders. "Yes. But remember, I asked you first."

"Prove it." He leaned forward and captured her lips. The kiss was gentle and loving. It coaxed and teased, asked, and took. Blay was truly hers. She released the worries and fears of the what-ifs and unknowns. She returned the love that flowed through their kiss.

CHAPTER 16

"I'm fine." Dawn leaned back. The creak of her chair at work sounded loud in the empty office.

"You didn't eat before you left, and it's almost dinner time. I've exercised the dogs with my new remote-controlled truck, and they've been fed and watered and walked. Thank you again for the truck, by the way."

She laughed at the thought of Blay playing with the dogs in the park. "I think you like it more than the pups do."

"I'll neither confirm nor deny that statement. But seriously, I'm going to pick up dinner for us from Brie's restaurant, so arguing doesn't matter," Blay answered in that no-nonsense tone he got when he felt he was right.

"I only have a couple of things to do before I can leave, and you shouldn't be carrying anything." She looked at the stack of folders and then at the clock.

"A couple of things? Isn't that what you said when you left this morning? And I have a perfectly good hand to carry a takeout bag."

"I think I said a few, which is more than a couple," she laughed. "All right. Call me when you get here, and I'll come to the front and let you in."

"Anyone else working today, or will we have the building to ourselves?"

"I saw the one guy from IT leave about ten minutes ago. So, I don't think anyone else is here. At least there are no cars in the parking lot." She stood and worked her way over to the window. "Oh, Peggy just pulled up."

"Peggy?"

"I told you about her. She's the new HR specialist. She must be decorating her office."

"What makes you say that?"

"She's carrying a big box. Probably plants or something." Dawn glanced at the documents that were supposed to have gone to her for processing but still sat on her desk. "I have a ton of work to offload on her. I'm glad she came in today. This way, I can answer any questions she may have."

"All right, I'll let you go then. I'm going to see if Brie is around. She's called every day since they let me loose from the hospital. She's always been a mother hen."

"Take your time and tell her I said hello."

"Will do. I love you."

"I love you, too." She smiled and looked down at the toe of her sneaker as she spoke. The words were too precious to say without thinking how they'd changed her life. She pushed 'End' and turned back to her desk. With renewed energy, she sat down and sent an interoffice memo to Peggy asking her to come by the office when she had time. After that, she dove into the rest of her mandatory to-do list. The shadows lengthened as she worked.

"You rang?"

Dawn jumped and clutched her chest. "Oh, crud, Peggy, you startled me."

The woman held her arms behind her back and glared at her. "We're the only ones in the building."

Taken aback by the woman's anger, she nodded, glancing at the clock. "Yeah, Mark from IT left about forty-five minutes ago."

"Good." Peggy shut the door with her foot.

Dawn swiveled in her chair and made a move to stand up. The gun in Peggy's hand stopped the motion.

She pushed back in her chair, knocking the back against her desk. "What the hell?"

"Shut the fuck up," Peggy screamed at her.

"Peggy, what's the matter?" Dawn couldn't understand the woman's hostility.

"Stop calling me that!" the woman screamed at her. The vein on her forehead bulged and her face was red. "My name is not Peggy. My name is Ellen!" The gun shook in the woman's hand. "You stole him from me. You stole him from my baby!"

"But you're not pregnant!" Dawn stated the obvious fact. Peggy, or Ellen, whoever, was rail thin.

"I was. I was pregnant. You can't tell me I wasn't!" the woman shouted at her. "He was mine. I was pregnant."

"What happened to the baby?" Dawn swallowed hard after she asked, but dear Lord, please, don't let this woman have hurt that child.

"I lost it two weeks after Blay told me he wanted a paternity test." The woman seemed to remember she had a gun in her hand and motioned toward Clyde's office. "He loves you. Everyone loves you. Everyone thinks you're special. I was special. I was pregnant. He didn't want me. What makes him want you?"

Dawn flicked her eyes toward Clyde's office. "I don't know how to answer that. I don't know you. Wait, you were pregnant when you went to Blay's parents' house."

"A stage prop! It cost twenty bucks online." Ellen bared her teeth in a feral growl. "He can't have you. When he realizes that, he'll come back to me."

The pungent odor of smoke reached Dawn. "What have you done?" The blaring sound of the building's fire alarm pierced the office.

"Did you know this building is in Blay's station's catchment area? That means he'll come. That means he'll come and save me. He'll see it then. *You* started this fire. *You* started this fire just like you started the fire at your house. You're doing it for sympathy. You're doing it to trap him. He'll figure that out. Especially when he finds me here." Ellen laughed, but the laughter had an unhinged sound of someone who had lost their mind.

Dawn's phone was just inches from her finger-tips. She pushed the chair ever so slightly. "Blay isn't working today."

"Liar! I know his schedule. I know when he

works." Spittle flew from the woman's mouth as she shouted.

"He had surgery on his hand. When he fell through the floor, he was at the hospital!" Dawn shouted the answer at the woman. She was done playing nice. She was done being threatened. A vice-like grip of anger tightened deep inside her. The woman in front of her had threatened her and the man she loved for the last time. Dawn stood up and grabbed for her phone.

"Put it down. Put it down now, or I'll shoot you." The woman's hand shook so violently there was little likelihood she could pull the trigger.

Dawn lifted the phone. Ellen grabbed the gun with both hands and screamed. The echoing percussion of the gun firing was the last sound Dawn heard.

Blay saw the dark cloud of smoke as he turned down the access drive to Clyde's immaculate new office building and logistics hub. He floored the gas and drove like a bat out of hell down the drive. "Fuck, no, no, no!" Blay slammed on the brakes, jerked open the door to his truck, and dropped down to the blacktop. He could hear sirens in the distance. It had to be his crew. He ran to the office but couldn't open the front door. The damn entry system. He used his good arm to pull a landscaping rock from the flowerbeds. Using the forearm of his bad hand, he carried it to the door and chucked it at the glass; it shattered but didn't break. Blay used his foot to break through the sheet glass. As he entered, he heard the fire trucks turning down the access point. The smart play would have been to wait, but he didn't care. He had to get Dawn out.

Where was she? *Think! Damn it, King, think! She said she could see Peggy carrying a box...* Blay glanced out the door and noticed a car parked by his truck and Dawn's SUV. *The front of the building.* He raced down the hall and turned left at the first corridor. Smoke rolled toward him from the back of the building. He covered his mouth with his T-shirt and kept going, checking door after door. There was nobody in any of the offices. Finally, he reached the corner and kicked in the door without any warning.

There, lying face down in the middle of the office on the floor, was Dawn.

"You found me!"

His eyes snapped to the right.

"Ellen? What?" *Whatever.*

He needed to get to Dawn. He made a move toward her.

"Stop! Don't go to her! This is all her fault. She's trying to steal what's mine. She took your attention away from our baby and me. That's why my baby's gone." The woman held a gun in her hand. It was pointed at Dawn.

Blay froze no more than six feet from Dawn. He turned his full attention to Ellen. Ellen was wearing skintight jeans and a form-fitting shirt. He tried to understand, but it was too early for her to have had the child, wasn't it? "What did you do?"

"What did I do? I loved you. That's what I did. That's all I did. I loved you. I wanted your baby. You didn't!" Ellen screamed at him.

"Where is the baby, Ellen?" His gut flipped.

"I lost it. I lost the baby, and you didn't care." The woman's face contorted into a snarling mess.

"I didn't know!" Blay inched closer to Dawn. Dark smoke entered from the open doorway and filled the office. He knew his crew was outside the building but had no idea what Ellen would do if someone else entered the office.

Ellen laughed; it was a sickening sound. "Because of her." Ellen stood up from the chair she'd been sitting in. "She just won't go away. I shot her. I had

KRIS MICHAELS

to. I wanted you to see that she was pathetic. I wanted you to see that she couldn't give you what I can. Why can't you see that you're mine? Answer me!"

Blay turned to look at Dawn again. He didn't see any blood. He turned his attention back to the maniac with a gun. "I never thought about you. I didn't even remember your name when you called to tell me you thought the baby was mine. I'm very careful. I always wear a condom, and I always check to make sure they held. We screwed twice. Nothing more. We don't even know each other." He moved toward Dawn as he spoke, but he wasn't close enough. He had to figure out a way to get to her to help her.

Ellen screamed in rage. She lifted the gun and pointed it at him. Blay moved on instinct. He lunged forward and slapped the weapon out of Ellen's hand with his wrapped, injured hand. The gun flew to the corner of the room, and Ellen attacked him. The woman bit, kicked, scratched, and fought like a wild woman. Blay did everything he could to subdue her without hurting her. Finally, he twisted her arm behind her back and muscled her to the floor. "Stop it!" Blay only had one good hand to hold the insane woman. He put pressure on her arm with his knee as he unfastened his belt and wrapped it around Ellen's arms, threading the buckle into a slot. He tightened it and fed the flap through the buckle.

He scrambled to Dawn. The smoke stung his eyes, but he carefully examined the woman he loved. Her pulse was strong. There was no blood, so he turned her over. A streak of blood was smudged down her cheek, originating from a massive knot on her forehead, but he could see no other injuries.

Smoke billowed into the office. Ellen's screams and curses were muffled as she struggled to get out of the hastily rigged restraint.

They needed clean air *now*. He coughed when he inhaled. Moving to the window, he grabbed an office chair and slung it with one hand toward the glass. The damn thing bounced off the thick pane.

He heard his crew before he saw them. "In here! Three in position one corner office!" He dropped the chair he'd just hefted with his good hand.

"King?" He spun toward the door. He'd never been more grateful to see Royal in his life.

He coughed and held up a hand pointing toward Dawn. "Unconscious possible head injuries. I'll carry her out." He turned toward Ellen, intent on telling Royal she was a code 10-47 and needed to be turned over to the police.

The woman had freed herself and was crawling toward the corner where her gun had skittered. Blay sprinted toward the woman and half-tackled her as she reached the gun. The handgun fired; the percussion kicked Ellen's hand back. Blay grabbed at the weapon and it fired again. Ellen screamed, wrestling with him for control of the gun. She bit his good arm, biting down and tearing with a jerk of her head but not releasing. Royal appeared beside him, and his partner grabbed the handgun, twisting it from Ellen's grip, but the woman hadn't noticed. Blay's blood trickled down her chin.

"Grab her nose!" He shouted the words at Royal. The man's gloves came off, and he pinched Ellen's nose shut, trying to force the woman to open her mouth to breathe. Seconds ticked by, but Ellen continued to fight without oxygen, ravaging his arm. Finally, she released, and he fell backward. Royal pushed her to the ground and kept a hand on her upper back to keep her from getting away. "Rocker, we need backup in here. 10-47, two victims and the 10-47." Royal panted the words through the comms.

Blay walked on his knees over to Dawn. Coughing, he checked her pulse. He moved to pick her up, but Royal yelled at him from where he was keeping

Ellen down, waiting for backup. "Don't be stupid. You can't carry her out. I'll take her."

Three other members of his crew entered the office. Royal instructed them to take Ellen out, cautioning them that she needed to be handed over directly to the police. Royal strode over and bent to pick up Dawn, but Blay beat him. He slipped his good hand under her. The blood from his bite wound left a red smear on the floor and her clothes.

"Help me." He stared at Royal even as he coughed.

"If I get fired, you're going down with me." Royal helped to position Dawn in his arms. "The fire's under control. They're putting out the last of it. It started two halls over. I was heading out of the building when I heard you."

Blay nodded, and he and Royal made their way out of the building. He hustled Dawn over to the medics. "We got her, man," Keith Fontana, the lead EMT said as they swarmed her unconscious body.

"She's my fiancée."

A heavy hand landed on his shoulder. "Let them do their job." His Lieutenant's voice couldn't divert his attention from where Fontana worked on Dawn. "Let's get that arm looked at."

He nodded and stuck out his arm so Miller could

clean and bandage it. "Damn, man, was there a were-wolf in that building?"

"No, just a rabid woman." He glanced at his Lieutenant. "Sir, it was Ellen, my stalker. Ellen set the building on fire. She said she shot Dawn."

"No gunshot wounds, dude." Fontana shook his head. "She has a nasty bump to the head. The docs are going to want to see her. But there's no gunshot."

Blay released a lungful of air he didn't know he was holding in. "Thank God."

The captain motioned toward the ambulance. "You'll need to get that looked after, and no doubt, you'll have antibiotics out the ears. Human bites are vicious."

He turned to look at Rocker. "She's insane, sir. She completely lost any touch with reality."

"I can believe it. I'll lock up your truck. Get in the ambulance and go to the hospital. The police have that one under control."

Blay glanced over his shoulder. Ellen sat demurely in the backseat of a police car. She turned to look at him, and a sickeningly sweet smile spread across her blood-stained face. Blay couldn't help the disgust he felt. The woman was sick and he should feel pity or empathy for her situation, but he couldn't muster it. Not yet; maybe never. "Would you please tell the police I'll make a statement? She admitted that she shot Dawn. Even if she missed, the act should be charged as attempted murder."

"I'll pass it on. Now, get up on that bus and get to the hospital. Give me a call when you're clear." Rocker turned and headed back to the truck. Blay waited until the medical crew loaded Dawn into the ambulance and then, with a one-handed swing using the side handle of the ambulance, launched himself into the back with her. The move opened the bite, and red seeped through the white gauze that wrapped his arm.

He was pissed. They'd separated him and Dawn when they arrived, sending him to get his wound cleaned and sutured and taking her for evaluation. When he returned after filling out way too much paperwork and wasting time waiting for the doc to not only give him a shot of antibiotics but prescribe some too, the emergency room personnel refused to let him sit with Dawn.

She hadn't regained consciousness during the short ride to the hospital. His eyes traced the second-hand sweep of the clock in the waiting area.

Every minute they kept him from her drove him a little closer to the edge of his sanity.

When the sliding glass doors whooshed open for the millionth time since he'd arrived at the hospital, he'd perfected the art of ignoring them. Shiny black shoes stopped in front of him. His eyes lifted to the pressed gray slacks, black belt, gray vest, red tie, and crisp white shirt under a grey jacket. His father's somber face greeted him.

"How is she?"

Blay stood up, and his dad hugged him, careful not to touch his injuries. When they parted, Blay answered, "I don't know. Amber is her emergency contact. They won't even tell me if they got ahold of her yet. I left a voice message for Brody, told him what was going on, to get Amber here ASAP, and asked him to take care of the dogs until I could find out what is happening. Then I called Mom. She was unconscious, Dad. Ellen said that she shot Dawn. She started that fire. She started the fire at Dawn's house. She's not right. She's insane." Blay's voice shook as he spoke. Man, he was going to lose it if he didn't get some answers stat.

His dad motioned for Blay to take a seat and then sat down beside him. "We ran her fingerprints. Her name is Ellen Donahue. She has been in and out of mental institutions for the majority of her life. From the information I was able to glean from police reports since she came of age, this isn't the first time she's fixated on someone like this. There were two other incidents. We're holding her until we can get an official read on her competency. There are a lot of loose ends on this one. Depending on what the psychiatrists say, she might not stand trial for what she's done to you and Dawn."

"I don't care, Dad. I know she's sick. I hope she gets the help she needs. But she isn't my concern right now. Dawn is." He sent his gaze back to the nurse's station. He had to see her to know that she was okay.

"Let me go see what I can do." His father rose and walked over to the nurse's station at the same time that Amber flew through the emergency room doors.

Blay was out of his seat and with Amber in two seconds flat. "They won't let me in, Amber. They won't let me see her."

"Is she okay?" Amber's eyes swung from person to person before she leaned toward the desk. "I'm Amber King, Dawn Swanson's sister. What is her status?"

The nurse asked for identification before she

compared the name against the information on Dawn's emergency notification paperwork. "She's regained consciousness. The doctor has ordered a CT. She was taken upstairs about 25 minutes ago. I'll let you know as soon as she returns."

Blay closed his eyes. "This is all my fault."

"Bullshit." Amber whipped the response out. "This is a crazy woman's fault. Brody told me about the woman's past. She should be confined to a mental institution, not roaming the streets."

"I agree with your sister-in-law." His father slipped his hands into his slacks and rocked back on his heels. "Dawn's conscious. Right now, be thankful for that. It could have been so much worse. The Southeast District will be sending over a detective. I asked them to give me a half-hour with you before dispatching the unit. They'll want a statement from both you and Dawn."

Amber took a deep breath. She released it slowly, and he watched as she physically relaxed. "With Ellen in custody, at least we'll be able to get back to some semblance of normal." Her nose wrinkled. "Why do you smell like smoke?"

Blay rolled his eyes. "I ran into a burning building. It's what I do, you know."

Amber's eyes rounded wide. "Yeah, when you're

at work in full protective gear. With backup. And without a hand injury."

His father cleared his throat. "Again, I agree with your sister-in-law."

"Tell me either one of you would've done any different if it was Mom or Brody in there." He wasn't going to let them put on the high and mighty wardrobe. He knew each one of them would have risked their lives for the person they loved.

Amber stared at him and then narrowed her eyes. "True, but we are married. Are you trying to tell us something here?"

Blay stared at his sister-in-law and then at his father. "I love her. She loves me. I've asked her to marry me. Not that it's any of your business."

"Well, it is most certainly *my* business."

His mother's voice behind him pulled a groan from somewhere deep inside him. He turned around. "Hi, Mom." She reached for him, and he went into her arms. The hug was just as it always was: made from love. When he pulled away, his mom started the conversation, "Hi yourself. How's Dawn? What in the world happened to your arm?" His mom's gaze bounced from person to person.

"Dawn regained consciousness, but the doctor wanted to have a CT done. Yeah, Blay, what happened to your arm?" Amber cocked her head at him. "But wait, before you answer that, did you know Blay and Dawn were engaged?"

Blay dropped his head back on his shoulders and stared at the fluorescent lighting above him. He spoke to the ceiling. "Ellen bit me while we were wrestling for the gun."

"Gun?" Both Amber and his mother shouted the word.

He dropped his head and looked at both of them. "Yeah, the one she tried to shoot Dawn with. But, hey, here's an idea, why don't you all go bother Caitlyn about her lack of any relationship whatsoever? Yes, I'm in love. Yes, we are going to get married. No, I have no idea when, but does it really matter?"

"Well, if you ask the church, yes. But I'm not asking the church today. Today, we will concentrate on getting Dawn out of here and getting you back to the apartment to take a shower because, son, you stink. Then, when she's able, you and Dawn will come over to the house for dinner. *Then* I'll want all the answers." Hannah looked around. "It's been a long time since I've been to the emergency room. I normally end up in one of the surgical wards. Chauncey, be a dear and help me find a coffee machine. We'll need some to keep all of us going if my history in this place is any indication."

His father offered his mother his elbow. She slid her hand through it. His father's hand covered hers.

"Anything for you, my dear."

Blay watched them walk down the long corridor.

"That's the kind of love that lasts forever," Amber sighed as she watched them.

Blay nodded. "It's the kind of love they've taught us to find." He escorted Amber to the hard-as-hell plastic chairs. He lifted his eyes and noted the time.

How long does a CT take?

CHAPTER 17

It was official. She hated that woman. Her headache pounded to the point of nausea. She closed her eyes, blocking out the lights above her, but when she did, images of Ellen popped up, and she was in absolutely no mood to play whack-a-mole with visions of Ellen.

Finally, the door to the room they'd wheeled her into opened. "All right, the radiologist and I looked at the scan. We didn't see anything abnormal. I'll prescribe you some pain meds for that headache. Do you have people here?" The doctor's voice was way too loud and way too cheery.

She opened her eyes, swallowed hard, and stared at the doctor. "Blay." She croaked out the word. "Blay

King." She had no idea how she'd gotten here, but every cell in her body knew he'd be here, waiting to see her.

"I'll have the nurse bring him in. In the meantime, you rest, and we'll look at discharging you in the morning. That blow to the head was significant."

She snorted, "You're telling me."

The doctor laughed. "Guess that was rather redundant after the CT, wasn't it?"

"Just a bit."

She was rewarded with another low rumble of laughter. "I'll work on that. I'll check on you before the end of my shift and in the morning when I come on duty. If you've had a quiet night, we'll discharge you as long as you have someone at home to take care of you."

She smiled as much as the hydraulic-powered jackhammer in her head would allow. "I do." She had Blay.

The doctor left, the nurse came in, and with her came the blessed pain medication. "We have something here for nausea and the pain, but we're going to give them to you intravenously, so I'm going to set up the IV stand then get you going with these meds."

Her headache was so intense she barely felt the

IV inserted into the back of her hand. "Can I see Blay now?"

The nurse nodded. "Is he here at the ward or in the ER?"

She opened her eyes. "I don't know. But please, I need to see him."

The nurse smiled. "Don't worry, we'll find him. Close your eyes now and rest."

Like I have a choice? The light was killing her. She closed her eyes and swallowed hard, praying she wouldn't get sick. Moving her head right now would most definitely kill her. Dawn concentrated on her breathing, drawing it in and slowly releasing it. She was in pain, and then... she wasn't. Afraid to move in case the slightest twinge would bring back the pain, she remained still and drifted on the blessed relief from the overwhelming headache. Her body grew heavier, and she let herself drift to sleep.

She jolted awake. The lights were all out in her room except for a small light over the sink. She turned her head to the window and stared at the utter darkness.

"Hey."

She shifted again. "Blay?"

"Yeah, I'm right here." He unfolded his big body

from the chair shoved in the corner of the room. He took her hand when he reached her. "How are you feeling?"

Dawn gripped his hand and blinked as she took stock of the aches and pains. "My neck hurts when I turn it, but the headache is gone. Thank God. What happened? How did I get here?"

He lowered the silver guardrail and sat down beside her on the hospital bed. "What do you remember?"

She gripped his hand tightly. "Peggy, she's Ellen. How did she fake the references? I contacted them when I hired her."

He nodded. "In person?"

"No, email... Oh, hell, she spoofed the email addresses. I didn't give her any work to do, so of course, I didn't notice she wasn't an HR specialist. I can't believe I fell for that."

"You had no idea she'd do anything this desperate. What else do you remember?"

Dawn drew a deep breath. "She was going to shoot me. She set fire to the building. I tried to duck out of the way of the bullet. Then I woke up here. For the love of everything this side of hell, tell me that the cops have her in custody."

"In a manner of speaking, yes." Blay nodded.

"Okay, so, I'm not tracking right now, and I don't feel like playing twenty questions. Just spill it. Please?"

Blay gave her a half-smile. "Peggy is Ellen. There are a lot of gaps that the detectives are working on filling, but in a nutshell, she used a fake resumé to get the job with you when she realized that she couldn't get to me. Now that Sean has her fingerprints, he was able to confirm her prints were on the containers used to carry the accelerant into your house, so we know for a fact she set the fire that destroyed your home. Detective Meriwether was able to match partial prints found in our apartment. She was responsible for that, too. I got to the building right after you smacked your head on the corner of your desk. She thought you were dead, that she'd shot you. She went crazy when I told her I never loved her, that we didn't know each other."

"The baby? She said she lost it."

"That's what she told me, too. Hopefully, the doctors will be able to get the full story from her."

"Doctors? Was she hurt, too?"

"No. She has a history of mental illness. Dad was able to find that out once we had a positive ID on her. She's been placed under a psych watch. They need to determine if she's mentally competent to stand trial for the things she's done, including trying to kill you." He lifted his good hand to touch her cheek, drawing her attention to the bandage on his arm.

"What happened?"

Blay glanced down at the white gauze. "When I was wrestling the gun away from her, she flipped out. She bit down and tried to tear out a chunk of my arm. Royal got the gun, and we were able to get her to the cops." Blay rubbed the back of his neck with his good hand. "I've seen a lot of things working as a firefighter, but I've never seen anyone that far gone. It was… Damn. It was spooky."

She put her hand on his thigh. "This comes from a man that runs into burning buildings. She must have lost it."

Blay covered her hand with his. "She did, but she can't hurt us anymore."

"You saved me." She smiled at him.

"You should have never been in that position. It was my fault you were."

"Bullshit. It was a crazy woman's fault."

Blay barked out a laugh. "That is exactly what Amber said."

Dawn stroked his hand with her thumb. "Good, glad someone else agrees with me."

"Sean stopped by when we were waiting for you. He said one of your ex-employees had confessed to damaging your car. They got a hit on him when he was thrown in jail for his third DUI in a month."

"Is it bad that I'd forgotten about the car? With everything else that's been happening I hadn't given it a second thought."

"Sean's a perfectionist. No way he'd let that detail go without running it to the ground."

"We have good friends and family."

"The best." He leaned down and kissed her on the forehead.

She sighed and smiled up at him. "The doctor said I could come home tomorrow."

Blay chuckled. "I believe what he said was that if you had a good night tonight, he'd see about discharging you tomorrow. Amber talked to him, and she let me be present. We both need to change our emergency contact information. Oh, and I may have let it slip that we're engaged."

Dawn adjusted her head a bit on the pillow, wincing at the pull of muscles in her neck. "To who?"

"Well, Amber and…"

"And?"

"My dad and my mom." Blay leaned forward and kissed her. "Sorry, I was so damn mad that the nurses wouldn't tell me a thing, and I was worried out of my mind. I just kind of... blurted it out."

"Blurted it out." Dawn closed one eye and looked at him. "Umm... okay." It didn't matter to her who knew, but she wasn't going to have anyone start planning their wedding. There was plenty of time for that.

Blay's eyes narrowed. "Okay?"

She shrugged and gasped. "Shit... Note to self: don't shrug."

"Do you want me to get the nurse?" Blay was on his feet and heading to the door.

"No, no, I'm fine. Really." He paused and looked at her. She wiggled her fingers at him. "Come back. I'm fine, just sore." He retraced his steps and carefully sat down on the mattress.

"I don't care who knows that we're engaged, but we need to find a normal before we make any plans. I want to know what it's like to have a routine with you, to find our groove before anyone shoves us toward the altar. I'm going to marry you but on our schedule. Not Amber's, not your mom's. Our schedule."

Blay chuckled. "If anyone can hold off Hover Mother, it's you."

Dawn smiled and let her heavy eyelids drop. "She's wonderful."

She felt Blay lean down and kiss her forehead. "She is, and so are you. I love you."

"I love you more."

EPILOGUE

hree Years Later:

Dawn draped the soft pink cashmere blanket over the crib railing. Her hand went to her massively big belly as it hardened. She blew out the air in her lungs slowly, counting the length of the contraction. It passed, and she glanced at the clock. Ten minutes apart. She'd wait until they were at five minutes or her water broke before she woke up Blay. The doctor had said first babies were notoriously stubborn and often delayed their arrivals. Opening the bundle of diapers, she put several on the changing table and opened the baby wipes, setting them next to the diapers. She opened the small drawer under the changing table—everything she'd ever need, thanks to the baby shower a month ago.

"What are you doing up?" Blay's hair was standing up on one side, and his eyes were barely open. Thor and Odin lifted their heads from where they'd laid down when she came into the room they'd converted to a nursery.

"Just checking that everything is ready." She turned back to the changing table and then looked at the crib.

"Of course, it's ready. You've been working in here for the last week. Our little girl has everything she needs." Blay walked up behind her and wrapped his arms around her belly just as another contraction hit. "Oh, shit. You're having contractions." His hands splayed over her belly as he started counting. She blew out the air, and when it stopped, they glanced at the clock at the same time. "How far apart?"

"It was ten." She lifted her eyes to his. "But that was only four."

"Four minutes? Oh, my God. Get the bag. No, wait, I'll get the bag. I need to get you a jacket. Or a robe? Do you need a robe? Do we need to call the doctor?" The dogs jumped up and started to prance around. Thor barked and charged out of the room, heading to the front door.

"Blay."

"Shit, sit down. No, wait, don't sit down, let's get to your car. I'll come back for the bag."

"Blay!" She bent over, her body tightened, and fluid ran down the inside of her legs. Blay was beside her in a second. Gone was the crazy husband; instead, her emergency responder was entirely in charge now, which allowed her to be just a bit frightened.

Blay picked her up and took her into their bedroom. "I'll be right back; I'm going to put the dogs in the bathroom." She nodded and rubbed her belly, watching as he ushered the dogs into the bathroom and shut the pocket door. He was back in an instant and helped her get out of her wet nightgown. "I'm going to take a look, babe. If you've been in labor for a while, the baby may be closer to coming than we thought." She lifted her legs and felt him as he examined her. "Okay, well, we have good news and bad news."

"Oh, gawd!" The contraction hit her like a ton of bricks. "Ahgg!" She grabbed Blay's hand.

"Babe, don't push. *Do not push.* Pant, pant through it. I need to get some things before you push." Blay talked her through the contraction, and then he was gone. She heard him on the phone in the hallway.

"That's right. Thank you, I'll put you on speaker in just a minute."

He came back with a stack of towels from the linen closet and lifted her bottom, laying three under her. "This is so we can clean away the fluid as it accumulates. I'm going to pour some alcohol over the scissors, and we're going to try to wait for the medical response crew to arrive. Okay?"

She shook her head. "Blay." Another contraction came fast, and it was a doozy. She grabbed his hand. The contraction pulled a groan-slash-scream from her, even though she was really trying not to push. "I have to push. I have to!" She had no idea how she knew that, but she did.

"Okay, love, okay. I've done this before, and we have help on the way. Give me two seconds to unlock the front door and grab the rubbing alcohol from the medicine cabinet in the kitchen. Pant, just like you learned in class. Pant with me." She concentrated on him and panted. He slipped off the bed. Freaking out wasn't an option, but God, she was going to do it. *She was supposed to have their girl in the hospital. With doctors. Oh, God!* She panted harder.

Blay was back and snapping on blue latex gloves. "I can see her hair. She has really dark hair." Blay ran his hand down her leg. She felt him as he rounded the bottom of her birth canal with his fingers.

"Blay!" Another contraction hit.

"Okay, let's get our little miss out into the world. Grab your legs here." He positioned her hands. "When you feel the urge to push, I want you to bear down."

She did, gasping for air after the effort.

"That was good, baby. Really good." Blay talked her through the pain and the pushing. "Okay, yes, that's it. Here she is."

As he said the words, two men jogged through the bedroom door. "Give me a brief."

Blay smiled at her. "The professionals are here, sweetheart. She just delivered the head, no umbilical cord issues."

"Blay!" Her belly contracted again.

His focus was back on her. "It's okay, babe, one more good push, and we'll have the shoulders, and she'll be here. Bear down."

Dawn did as he told her, and minutes later, her daughter was born. The other men were busy with medical equipment and radios while Blay coached her through the delivery. Once she landed in his hands, they moved quickly. One tied off the umbilical cord as Blay held their daughter in a hand towel.

Dawn panicked. "She isn't crying. Why isn't she crying?" She reached for her baby.

The other man leaned over and suctioned out her nose. A strong wail immediately echoed around the bedroom. Blay brought the baby to her and placed her on Dawn's chest, draping them both in towels. It was only then she realized she was naked, but there were no emotions to be spared on embarrassment. Her heart grew in love and amazement while she stared at the wonder of their daughter.

A perfect baby. Absolutely perfect.

"She's beautiful, just like you." He kissed her and their daughter.

The rest of the time at the house was a blur. She kept the baby even as she delivered the placenta. The men that responded took the baby for a short time to get her vitals, and Blay dressed her in a new nightgown and lifted her onto the gurney, placing their baby back on her chest.

Brody was standing in the hall and spoke as she was ushered down the stairs. "I made the calls for you, brother. Congratulations to both of you. I told them all to wait until you called them to come to the hospital. We'll take care of everything here."

Blay said something in response, but she couldn't

say what, she was lost in the marvel of their daughter.

Her OB walked into the room the hospital had assigned her. "Dawn, are you trying to put me out of business?"

"No, but my husband might be." She smiled at her doctor and pointed in Blay's direction.

Blay snorted. "Not on your life. Fire is less frightening and less messy." He was holding their daughter, rocking back and forth a bit.

"I guess it is good to have a first responder for a husband, just in case," the doctor chuckled and lowered his voice as he walked over to the baby and tucked the swaddling under their daughter's chin. "She's beautiful. The emergency room doc told me you both came through with flying colors. How long were you in active labor?"

"Not long, that's why I didn't come in. I woke up about two, and they were fifteen minutes apart. Not long after, they were ten, and they were pretty consistent at ten for about an hour. I was going to wake up Blay at five minutes apart, but they went from ten to four, and then boom, there she was."

"Well, congratulations. Next child, if you have a twinge, come in. I talked to your pediatrician. Your little one is doing wonderful, and we can release both of you today. Will you have help at home?"

Dawn chuckled. "She has so many aunts and uncles, but they'll have to get past Grandma Hannah and Grandpa Chauncey."

Blay glanced over at her. "Do you think they'll let us have a day without being swarmed?"

She thought of each of Blay's brothers and sisters, of the McBrides, who were just as close as family, Chauncey, and of Hannah, who was indeed the best mother-in-law in the world. Dawn smiled at her husband, the man she loved more than she could ever have imagined. "Our family? Not a chance."

The End

ALSO BY KRIS MICHAELS

Kings of the Guardian Series

Jacob: Kings of the Guardian Book 1

Joseph: Kings of the Guardian Book 2

Adam: Kings of the Guardian Book 3

Jason: Kings of the Guardian Book 4

Jared: Kings of the Guardian Book 5

Jasmine: Kings of the Guardian Book 6

Chief: The Kings of Guardian Book 7

Jewell: Kings of the Guardian Book 8

Jade: Kings of the Guardian Book 9

Justin: Kings of the Guardian Book 10

Christmas with the Kings

Drake: Kings of the Guardian Book 11

Dixon: Kings of the Guardian Book 12

Passages: The Kings of Guardian Book 13

Promises: The Kings of Guardian Book 14

The Siege: Book One, The Kings of Guardian Book 15

The Siege: Book Two, The Kings of Guardian Book 16

A Backwater Blessing: A Kings of Guardian Crossover

Novella

Montana Guardian: A Kings of Guardian Novella

Guardian Defenders Series

Gabriel

Maliki

John

Jeremiah

Guardian Security Shadow World

Anubis (Guardian Shadow World Book 1)

Asp (Guardian Shadow World Book 2)

Lycos (Guardian Shadow World Book 3)

Thanatos (Guardian Shadow World Book 4)

Tempest (Guardian Shadow World Book 5)

Smoke (Guardian Shadow World Book 6)

Reaper (Guardian Shadow World Book 7)

Hope City

Hope City - Brock

HOPE CITY - Brody- Book 3

Hope City - Ryker - Book 5

Hope City - Killian - Book 8

Hope City - Blayze - Book 10

STAND ALONE NOVELS

SEAL Forever - Silver SEALs

A Heart's Desire - Stand Alone

Hot SEAL, Single Malt (SEALs in Paradise)

Hot SEAL, Savannah Nights (SEALs in Paradise)

Hot SEAL, Silent Knight (SEALs in Paradise)

ABOUT THE AUTHOR

USA Today and Amazon Bestselling Author, Kris Michaels is the alter ego of a happily married wife and mother. She writes romance, usually with characters from military and law enforcement backgrounds.

Made in the USA
Las Vegas, NV
13 October 2021